The First Time She Fell

To Gloria

Thanks

Cacob

THE FIRST TIME SHE FELL. Copyright © 2011 by Caleb Ludwick. All rights reserved; all design content is owned by the respective designers, and used with permission. See Acknowledgements for credits. Early versions of the texts of "Swim" and "Underlay" were published online in 2003. No part of this book may be used or reproduced in any manner whatsoever without written permission, except in the case of brief quotations embodied in critical articles and reviews. For information address 26 Tools llc at http://26tools.com.

Printed in the USA.

ISBN: 978-0-615-57130-0

The First Time She Fell
8 short stories in the visual and verbal

CALEB LUDWICK

WITH DESIGN BY MICHAEL HENDRIX, BEN HORNER,
MANDY LAMB MEREDITH, NICK DUPEY, LIZ TAPP,
ROBY ISAAC, JOSEPH SHIPP AND BETH JOSEPH

cover design by Paul Rustand of Widgets & Stone

to kgl

My in-love, promise me yourself,
And then forgetting that, remember me –
Me? Forget remembering that, then, and
Love my promise, yourself in me.

Contents

What Marinela Didn't Say   1
DESIGN BY MICHAEL HENDRIX
Location Director, IDEO · Boston MA

Patete   22
DESIGN BY BEN HORNER
Creative Director, Papercut · Chattanooga TN

The Houses Under the Sea, the Dancers Under the Hill   50
DESIGN BY MANDY LAMB MEREDITH
Design Director, Scout · Birmingham AL

Thin King Blues   88
DESIGN BY NICK DUPEY
Communication Designer, IDEO · Boston MA

Underlay   90
DESIGN BY LIZ TAPP
Owner, Liz Tapp Design; Publisher, Mule Magazine · Knoxville TN

Cuntata 82   129
DESIGN BY ROBY ISAAC
Creative Manager, Mannington Commercial; Partner, iV Design · Philadelphia PA

Swim   176
DESIGN BY JOSEPH SHIPP
Communication Designer, IDEO.org · San Francisco CA

All the Way to LAX   193
DESIGN BY BETH JOSEPH
Graphic Designer, True North · Chattanooga TN

Author's Note   212
Acknowledgements   214

that it's better to
make a bad choice
for good reasons,
than a good choice
for bad reasons.

Even in the late cool of a Saturday, the kitchen is hot as noon. He walks through the swinging doors and sees her flushed at the open ovens, flour ribboning the light from the window. Stops short, wondering if she might take him by the hand and lead him along leafy streets to a first-floor efficiency, her backward glance insolent, secret, unafraid.

He says her name, and then something about maids, and waitresses, and servant girls; that she is wearing that apron like an invitation. And Marinela Constancia Ruiz hears him.

What Marinela didn't say:

- that maybe it's better to make a bad choice for good reasons, than a good choice for bad reasons.

- that 'Fingers with wedding bands stir a bitter batter' was a favorite saying of her mother.

- that the reason her mother, Señora Immaculata Vegas Ruiz, broke the custom of perpetuating family names should be obvious. After all, her own mother's own mother had broken the custom first, naming Immaculata Vegas after the local chapel and the bright postcards of Las Vegas — with the disastrous result that Vegas had seven children by four different visiting American businessmen.

VEGAS

So Immaculata Vegas, believing that naming can go a long way in either direction, had named Marinela after the brand of her favorite store-bought pastry. Brown outside but inside white, she would say. You might look dark as chocolate and inside be white as sweet cream filling, but never forget you can't be both. That in America, you'll never be either.

- that she had overheard Buckley's father tell him to clear dishes. His exact words (Marinela has an excellent memory) were: "Despite the presence of hired help, the groom should be host, sponsor and servant. All things to all people." So when Buckley pushed through the swinging doors with plates for the sink, she knew he was there not because he is a gentleman, but because he is a child.

- that she saw him stop resenting his father the moment he saw her, sweating in her apron. He grinned at her as if they'd never met, as if the cracked and yellowed ceiling was about to collapse on him in a settling haze of happiness.

- isn't this a grand party? Look at the chairs pushed against the wall for dancing, and a cake with three tiers and enough icing to make anybody happy. Groomsmen pretending to be adults pretending to be teenagers; boys in cummerbunds cupping beers and smoking cigars and cursing, their Tennessee down-South

- 4 fresh mint springs
  2 shots Bookers
  1 t powdered sugar
  2 t water
  Crushed ice

mouths tonguing the words like bleached teeth —
nothing like when Tampico boys talk rough and tumble.

Boys in girls in bathrooms and coat closets. Boys
snatching handfuls of food from warming trays.
Their mothers in pastel wide-brimmed hats that
hang low over their eyes.

- that she speaks excellent English because she grew
  up five miles from Mexico's first Coca-Cola
  bottling plant (est 1926). That the Southern brown
  sugar bubble water is as much in her blood as his.
  But that sometimes it is better to pretend she can't
  hablo ingles. Or speaking, not understand. Or
  understanding, not really understand.

- that her apron might be stained, but the cloth is
  two layers of canvas with a waterproof fabric sewn
  between. So he need not worry about her blouse.

- welcome back to the Wilhoit Street Reception Hall.
  Though she scarcely has the right to welcome guests,
  it being only her second month. On the other
  hand, every man and woman coming into the
  kitchen notices only her, so she might as well be
  appointed welcoming committee.

The two other cooks, Jaione and Jasmine, have each worked at the Hall for more than thirty years, while she herself is not thirty years old, or twenty-five, or even twenty-two. That she had been hired just after Easter, when Miss Emmeline died at the age of 81. From what the others say, Miss Emmeline suffered a stroke while driving home on the Interstate, her hands gripping the wheel of her Pontiac in a heroic act, steering her car out of traffic. Her car rolled to a standstill on the grass and gravel shoulder. The burning sun crept toward the tailgate. When the police arrived, they thought Miss Emmeline was waiting for a grandchild who had gone to sit on his heels among the pines. They stopped only because the exhaust was spouting great clouds of dry smoke.

- that Easter is a wonderful holiday in America, whatever that business about the rabbit.

- that he reminds her of a man from Alabama, who came down to Tampico looking for low wage labor, who had dressed a hundred of them in print shorts and tank tops and boarded them onto a leased Carnival cruise ship. Sailed straight into the Puerto de Mobile smeared with sunscreen and coached on how to act drunk and entitled. Kids were given blow-up toys. Young mothers gagged infants and tucked them into hollow watermelons with tiny air holes to keep the crying sounds inside until they were reborn, sticky sweet, into America.

The border patrol was too busy hunting illegals to worry about a cruise ship of bitchy tourists, so they walked straight up Government Street and onto construction sites. But Marinela and her sisters and their mother kept walking all the way to the bus stop, all the way to Chattanooga. Following that brown bubble sugar water flowing like a lifeline between home and home.

- that on the long bus ride her mother had gathered everyone together to say that she had no legacy to give, other than the ability to smile and endure with the passion and patience of a portrait; saying that this is not how things should be, or could be, or perhaps even will be, only how they are.

- that her first week in Chattanooga, a man saw her in a Bi-Lo grocery store and offered her the role of the Virgin, in an Easter parade. The parade was where she first saw him, and shook his hand, and he offered her a job in the Men's Grille at the golf club. But that the following day, his fiancée arranged that she work instead at the Wilhoit Street Reception Hall.

- that she is an American, bona fide, with a favorite toothpaste, cartoon memories and a business plan, muchas gracias. That her children will have no accent, until they want one.

Ceci n'est pas sexy.
愛

- that he knows full well that her apartment is not on a leafy street but off a short city bus line, down a brown path that winds through back yards to a cinder block building passed over by the revival of Main Street. No fraud-mod balustrades decorate her building. That only a few years before, the apartment was squatted by dry-skinned alcoholic prostitutes who bummed cigarettes from the insurance workers downtown; but then the university launched an aggressive student exchange program, and within six months a venture capital firm out of Knoxville bought the building on the cheap and filled it with lipsticked Chinese sophomores drinking Fresca and wearing tee shirts silkscreened with MAYBE or CECI N'EST PAS SEXY.

- that it's the little things that get us through, because nothing doesn't seem too much to ask. Tiny mountains can only have tiny avalanches.

- that when he saw her at the Easter parade and wrote his cell phone number on her hand, she watched the ink spread into her palm's lines and creases like a future. Him, whose mother is Regent of the D.A.R., founder of the Junior League mentoring program, a Gold supporter of the Pops, Chair of the Christmas silent auction at the Y three years running. And her, whose mother is Señora Immaculata Vegas Ruiz. She had enjoyed imagining

CHEST

SKIRT

KNEES

the two mothers together in the tiny apartment,
over chiles en nogada, until she heard that in just
two weeks he would be married. Her sister had
called her common; but she, Constancia Marinela
Ruiz, had said there is no shame in being common.

- That when he came into the dark hotel bar, tan
  from boating, from all that sun on all that water,
  the pale sunglasses circles around his eyes made
  him look as if he looked all the world in wonder.
  That she had been suddenly aware of her knees
  showing under the brief skirt, small and vulnerable,
  of her black tee shirt tight across her chest, printed
  in block letters with FEED ME. FUCK ME. FINANCE ME.

  And, in case he didn't remember, that as he got
  drunk on tall cold bottles of beer he was already
  talking about horses.

- that Jasmine keeps a hat rack locked in the corner
  of the kitchen pantry, the hats all stolen from
  years of guests drunk on sangria. The week before
  Marinela left for Louisville, the three cooks pulled
  out the hats, choosing favorites in the burnished
  back of a pasta pot; made cucumber sandwiches and

mixed juleps; placed bets on ants running the windowsill. Jasmine clapping her hands; Jaione's cheeks rosy with cracked capillaries by years of oven heat and envy. Marinela laughing, the sound rolling up from her belly to spill out of her mouth, as easy as breathing.

that she had found the infield to be just like they say on the Internet. The Great Party of bourbon breath and blonde hair and round vowels, and thousands pressing in from every side, shouting and groping and passing out. Fireworks popping like synapses. By the third turn, boys pulling girls down to mud wrestle beneath the always clean, perfectly set, immense hats of bows and pastels and live flowers and silk trim and feathers that made her sneeze. That, when the race started, it seemed that the whole world was shouting together, their voices twisted in the air, braiding together under the thunder of hooves. And that with Buckley holding her hand so tight, she felt safe from slipping away in the crowd, being taken, being lost.

But then came the finish. Silence spread through the infield. And she, Marinela, had pushed through to the fence, away from his hand, and stood crushed against the railing while three men held the horse down as it tried to rise on shattered

forelegs, blood dark as lipstick against the pale bone. Its eyes were wild with filly fright as the jockey turned and walked away, not watching the veterinarian as he ran, with his long needle, toward the vein. And voices all around her had said: she got second, she ran damn fine. She ran like a locomotive, like a veteran, like a colt, like a muse.

- that she had walked straight to a bus stop and caught the long ride back to Lexington, to Knoxville, to Chattanooga. That she had been in the reception hall kitchen the next morning, before the sun came up. That she had watched him get married through the window, through the cool slant of Saturday sun.

- that she is not a pastry or a muse or a mare or a virgin or a Friday night white flight or Saturday stalker or enamorada or chucha cuerera or clutch or squeeze or flame or crush. That she is only waiting for him to leave, so she can go into the pantry to choose today's favorite hat. To laugh over the oven heat until tiny veins in her face pop, blushing.

So when Buckley is standing by the sink, watching as she washes plates, Marinela hears him talking but she is not listening. And so when he says, "It doesn't have to change. She doesn't have to know. You could come downtown with me tomorrow night. The men would bow, the women blush."

Marinela's pretty face
screws up into a question mark,

and she says nothing.

PATETE

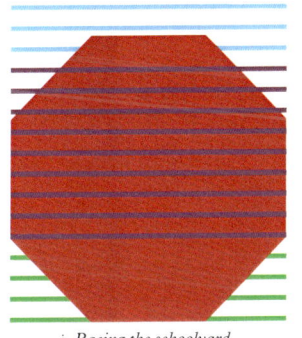

i. *Racing the schoolyard.*

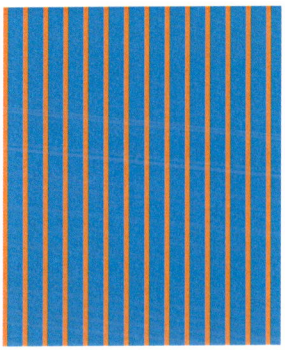

ii. *Summer swim.*

iii. *Dinnertime!*

iv. *A mother's errand.*

v. *Kissing at the creek.*

vi. *Lock and cock it.*

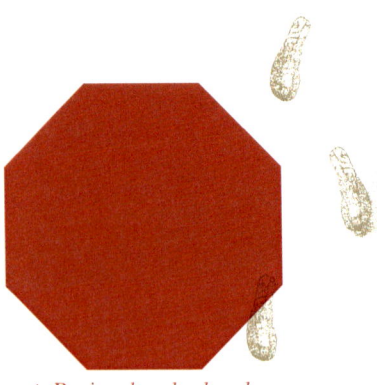

i. *Racing the schoolyard.*

He grew up with Lil, 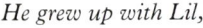 but never thought twice about her being a girl until the first time he saw her run. Not just run, but run fast – with a funny way of bringing her knees high at each step and holding her elbows in close, fists swinging like pistons.

He was in 5th grade; she was in 7th. He heard whispering in the school hallways before she did.

"Who do they say it was?" she asked. He tried to escape into the boy's bathroom but she followed him in. He looked from foot to foot on the cracked tile, the blackened grout.

"Nobody."

"You're a bad liar, Patete. How could it be nobody?" She was the first to call him Patete. It was French for little, she said, and she would stop when he was big enough to make her. Now everyone called him that.

So he told her what he'd heard: that it was Eric and Superchicken, two shooting guards from the JV. They said it was all her idea, that she drank until she saw stars and they had her at the paper recycling warehouse, on a pile of porn and crosswords. Lil got so angry she marched into 9th grade Geometry and called both of them to follow her outside.

"You want another go?" laughed Eric, and the class laughed with him. But the teacher, his bald head and mustache swelling, shouted until she closed the door.

She waited in the hall. When the bell rang, the whole class followed them outside, word spreading, picking up other kids as they went. Lil and the boys walked ahead, like tall somebodies the others would never be. Out the double exit doors into a parking lot frozen between an aluminum sky and claustrophobic concrete, smells of diesel and winter leaves.

"To the stop sign and back," she said.

Under his sweatshirt, Superchicken flexed his thin baller's biceps. Behind him, Eric shuffled and blew into cupped hands.

"Cmon Lil, it's cold. Let's just go inside," Eric said.

"You talk like a man, why don't you show it?"

"I'm not cold," said Superchicken. "Anybody hear me say I'm cold?"

"I'm cold," Eric said. "So let's do it or don't."

"One on one?" somebody asked, but Lil shook her head.

"Together. Like they say happened down at the recycling."

The boys bumped chests, laughed, then looked at her and thought better. Superchicken drew an invisible line with his foot.

"Ladies first, Lil."

"Don't you call me Lil."

Nobody said anything. After a few seconds, Patete said, quietly, "But Lil, that's your name."

"Shut up, Patete."

They started on a three count and when they reached the far stop sign, Lil was ahead by two strides. She was running harder than Patete had seen anyone run, ever. Her feet blurred the ground and she bit at the air, her eyes swollen from crying, her light skin flushing, her legs long as strings. But when they turned, the soles of her shoes slipped on loose ice and she went down with both hands splayed wide. The boys cornered expertly behind her and sprinted back toward the start.

Lil came up, her mouth a violent gash, her breath hot white. The huddled group backed away to clear a finish line just before Superchicken broke it, Eric neck and neck with him but Lil four steps back. She stood off to one side, her chest heaving, wiping long loops of spit from her mouth as Eric and Superchicken grinned around, pushing their way through the silent crowd to the rack where their Huffys were chained. Standing onto the pedals, they disappeared across the parking lot.

Patete followed Lil to the edge of the schoolyard, to a high metal fence – eight foot tall corrugated sheets of tin laced together with baling wire. She pushed at one of the wide panels, scraping it against the cold dirt until she could squeeze through. A few seconds later she swung it open again and looked out.

"What?"

"Is it true?"

"Does it matter?"

"Okay."

She's a girl and girls don't bite, Patete had heard, not unless you ask them to. He was afraid she might take a swing at him just for thinking it.

"You remember when we used to play in the creek, last summer?"

He nodded, slowly blinking, thinking of sun and shade.

"And after, we would eat watermelons we stole from the community garden? See who could spit seeds the furthest."

"I never did that."

"You don't remember?"

"That wasn't me. That must have been someone else," he said.

The tall fence panels spread in ripples left and right from where Patete stood, the metal clanging lightly under his knuckles.

"Maybe so,

" she said.

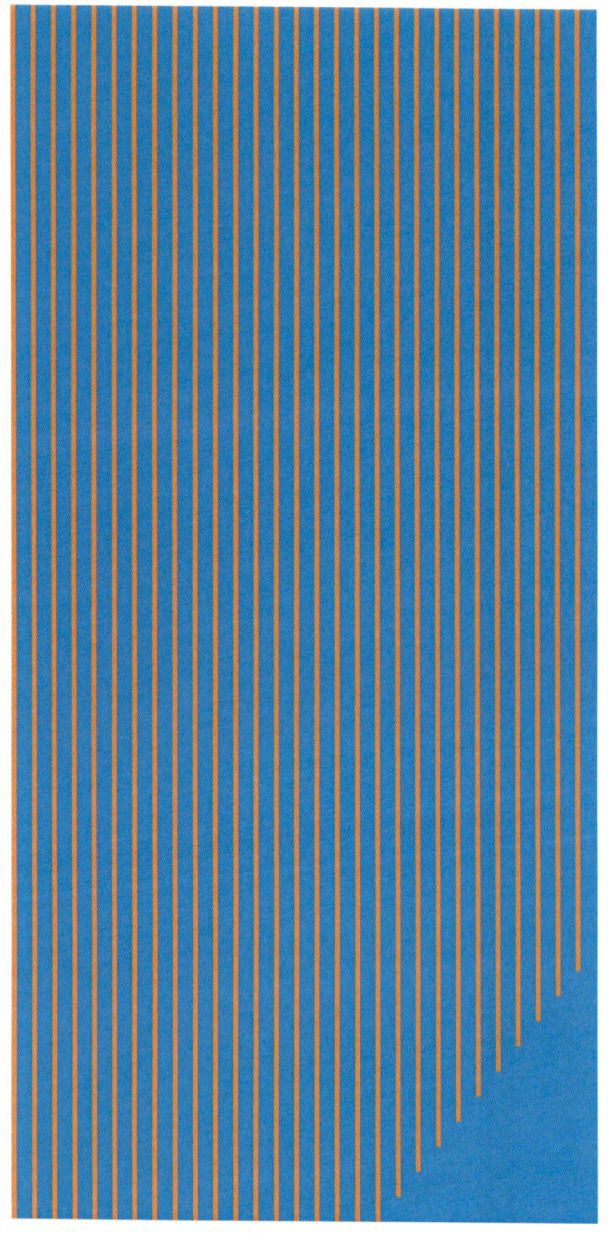

ii. *Summer swim.*

The summer before, on the last day of fourth grade, Patete had come outside to see saws and metal sheeting lying at the edge of the schoolyard. Lil's grandfather had died, somebody said, and her mother was using the insurance money to build a fence. So the man living with Patete's mother, a man he never called Dad, went down the block every day with his tools and the corrugated panels laid across a wheelbarrow. He worked loading docks at the Home Depot and when tin sheets got bent the manager would sell them off the pallet for two dollars each, cash only. He hammered the corners straight and built fences all over the neighborhood.

With so many sharp edges around, Lil's mother said it wasn't safe. So she sent Lil and Patete to play at the creek. They made the long walk along the tracks, balancing on the rails and telling jokes, throwing dirt clods to burst like dusty stars on the clanging boxcars. They stole cardboard boxes from the recycling plant and rolled them down a steep embankment to where the creek was knee-deep and brown. Lil ducked into the bushes to change into a bathing suit while Patete weighed the boxes down with stones. He watched flat-footed beetles walking on the creek's surface, shifting against the current, holding steady, gulping air. When Lil came out they jumped from the box tops to splash in the water, over and over until the boxes wet through and collapsed under them.

They went to the creek every day that summer – even after the fence was finished, even after the man left Patete's mother to move in with Lil's mother, even as Lil went deeper into the bushes to change, even as her bathing suit started to stretch and fill.

The last time they walked back to her house, the weekend before school began, Patete saw wet triangles showing through her clothes. She saw him looking and hit him, hard. He sat down, trying not to cry and waited for her footfalls to hush away before he followed. He walked past 50 gallon drums and abandoned washing machines that were scattered beside the tracks, behind buildings where dogs startled and yipped before disappearing under dumpsters. His hands bounced against his thighs. He squeezed through a chain link fence and out onto the Boulevard, up an alley, around a wide warehouse, kicking at a brick wall, his tennis shoes flicking dirt on his shirt. At the end of the alley he took two blind turns, then pushed through a door rusting in the open weather and was at the back of the school playground.

Lil was waiting for him at the fence. She held a panel open, and through it Patete could see the grass tall against the house, so tall that only the roof was visible.

"He never mowed our yard either. I had to do it."

"I could mow it if I wanted," she said.

"I hate mowing. It's boring."

"You're boring, and you can't come in."

Patete's face fell. "What? Why not?"

"He's here." She watched the house like it was watching her back. "You know, he can get the pills from Mexico that Mama needs. And she says he has needs, too." She shook her head. "Anyway, he has a car. He lets me drive it sometimes."

Patete thought about standing in the school locker room, surrounded by boys with hair showing on their arms and chests and between their legs – of how he never wanted to take his shirt off in the locker room, or around his mother, or anywhere except at the creek with Lil. And now, maybe not even there, not anymore.

"So see you tomorrow, I guess."

"Soon it'll be too cold to swim. I don't want to catch sick."

"We don't have to swim. We could throw rocks, or tell jokes," Patete said, lying: "I know some new ones."

"You know shit."

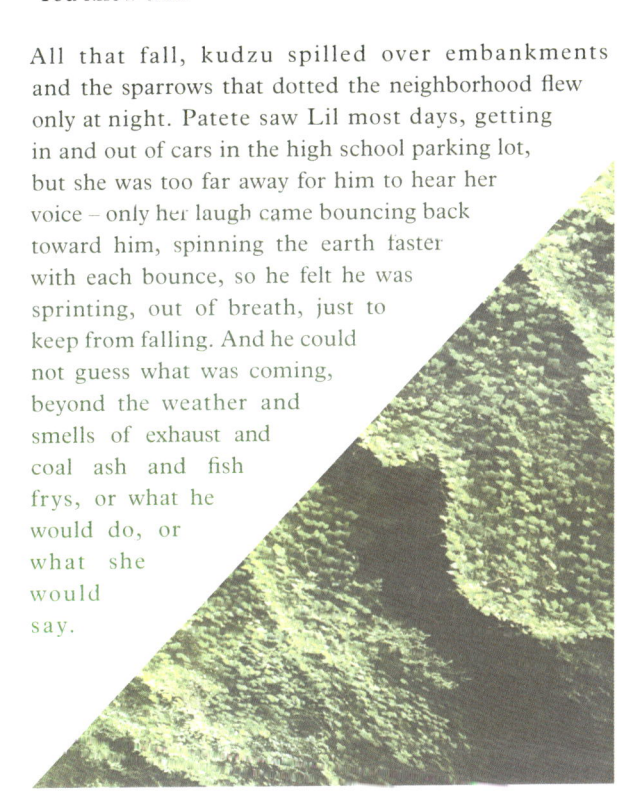

All that fall, kudzu spilled over embankments and the sparrows that dotted the neighborhood flew only at night. Patete saw Lil most days, getting in and out of cars in the high school parking lot, but she was too far away for him to hear her voice – only her laugh came bouncing back toward him, spinning the earth faster with each bounce, so he felt he was sprinting, out of breath, just to keep from falling. And he could not guess what was coming, beyond the weather and smells of exhaust and coal ash and fish frys, or what he would do, or what she would say.

The day before Thanksgiving, a police dispatcher chuckled at reports of a white man standing in the middle of Rossville Avenue, swinging a shotgun at the sky. When the patrol cars angled to a stop, their hands on sidearms, he shouted that he was tired of damn ducks skimming the rooftops, and wanted some dinner. The shotgun popped at his shoulder, echoing off the buildings around. Neighbors glanced at the windows, then went back to television.

But one duck jerked sideways, as if lassoed by an airy thread. It fell in a somersault, suddenly heavy, toward the ground before catching the air, its wings beating furiously. The band on its neck dripped as it jittered over three, four blocks before tumbling hard into the short grassy yards between two rows of identical houses.

From his window, Patete watched the duck land, green and white and brown and red into the grass. It stood on stick legs, one eye covered in dirt, its head looping a circle with each step, dragging its wing.

iii. *Dinnertime!*

As he watched, a front door opened and Mrs. Garcelle came out, holding a foot-long serrated bread knife. He knew her as a girthy woman, always on her front porch, and it seemed wrong to see her out in the yard in her house dress. Looking up, she saw him watching and held one finger to her mouth, shhhh, but farther down the street another door opened and another woman came out, shouldering bra straps into place, a rolling pin in her hand. The duck started waddling fast, arching one wing high, the other loose and useless. More doors opened. Men and women stalked the short walkways.

Patete sat at his window for a long time, for hours after dinner had been cooked and the dishes put away, waiting for morning to flood the world.

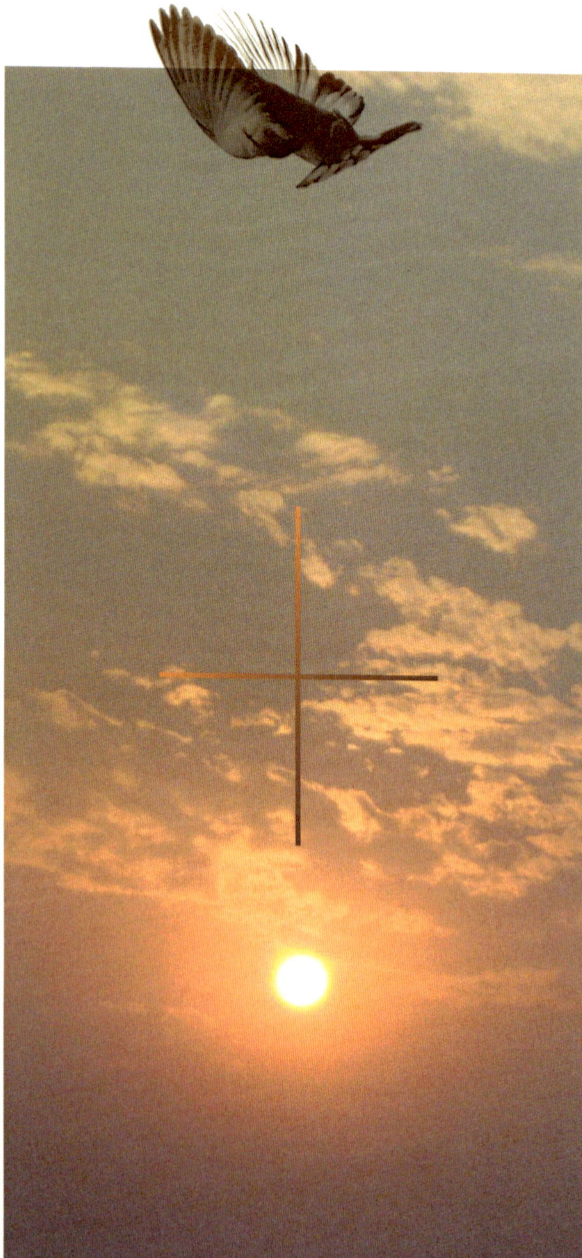

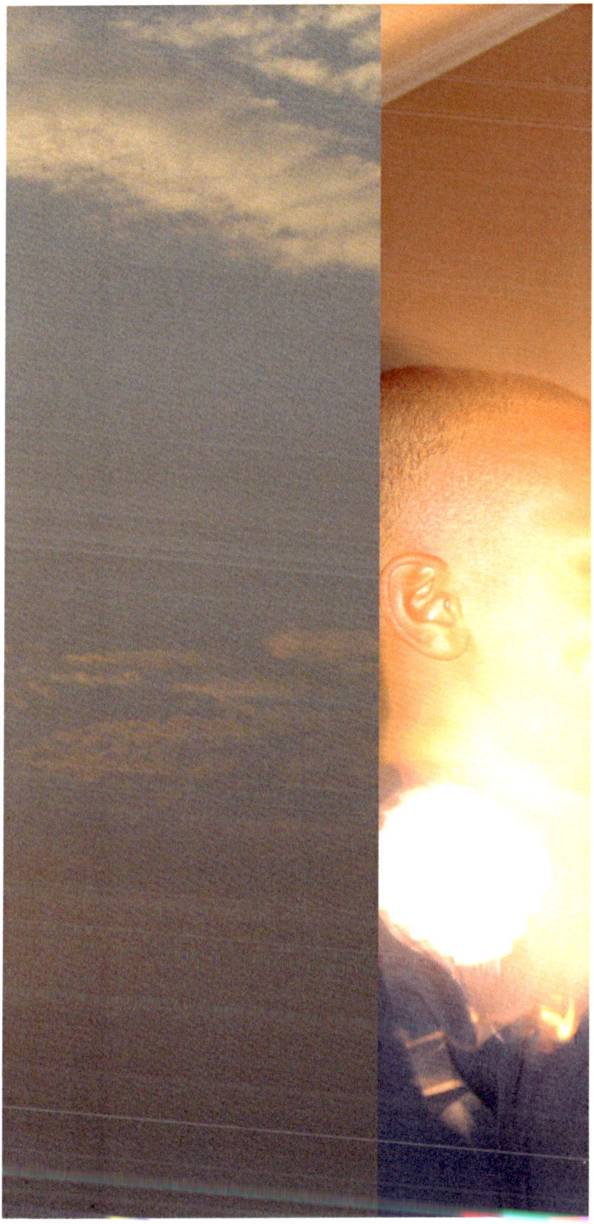

iv. *A mother's errand.*

His mother leaned back against the refrigerator door, a hazy ring of fingerprints and magnets over her head. Patete poked his head around the corner, grinning at her, his mouth making an unsteady butterfly shape that he never sees.

"I know what's in the fridge, Patete," she said from the floor. "Why didn't you clean it up? Is it milk?"

He nodded, still standing in the doorway.

"I don't want to know what happened," she said. "It doesn't matter when you stop being a child, Patete, or where, or even why. Only that it happens, and happens soon."

Beside her was a plate of half-eaten macaroni, smeared with orange cheese powder, crusting over. Patete could smell its stink from the doorway. She was still wearing the brown uniform unbuttoned over her undershirt, the security guard patch gaping like a loose flap of skin above her low breasts.

"Come sit with me, honey."

"I already ate. I had cereal."

"With milk. Don't I know it."

It was Saturday morning, the day after Lil's race. Patete wanted to tell her about Lil all but beating two boys, but he knew better; when his mom came from work, she was headed to bed. She patted the hard linoleum and he sat beside her, tucking his head under her arm. He leaned into her, rising and falling on her breathing.

"You know I'm proud of you baby. You let yourself in and lock up. You look after yourself all nights. But it's not enough, and I'm trying, but I just can't make do."

"I know," he said, not knowing.

She held her breath, half in half out, until he bounced his head on her chest and she exhaled, words rushing out of her mouth. "They say God is outside of time and place, Patete, so maybe there are things he can't remember. But I remember everything. And every time I pass that house I hate God like I hate him, and her, and even Lil, for stealing away the little bit of ease I'd gathered." She wiped her face. "I hate everything that won't stop the world turning long enough for me to jump clear."

Patete stared at her until she said, "No, baby, I don't really hate Lil. Not anymore."

He kissed her cheek and said, "Go to bed, mom. I'll go to the park."

"But maybe could you walk past her house on the way, first? Just one time."

She said it, touching his elbow. The same thing every Saturday – just one time, one walk past Lil's driveway to see if that old blue Honda was parked there. Maybe slip into the side yard, push at the fence panels to peek through. The man had caught Patete once, bending him across his naked knee like a father. But after Saturday after Saturday, Patete knew that her expression would be the same whether the Honda was there or not. Her bubble of strength would vanish without any noise at all, not even a popping sound, and there would be nothing for him to do but go into his room to play, and pray for her to stop crying, but she wouldn't, and wouldn't.

"I should be strong," she said; but he interrupted her, "I will."

"You're my good boy," she said thickly. "My man of the house."

But as soon as he was outside, Patete turned in the opposite direction. The street was bright, the sun suddenly warm again, without any of the ice or cold of the day before. Neighbors sat on porches or watching flickering televisions through open windows as children played with dogs on chains. Patete waited in line to buy Skittles at the 7-11, then went to the park bleachers to watch pick-up basketball. He sat on the foot slats, lining up the roundflat candy on the empty beach in front of him, row by row by color.

Groups of three and four were already playing at each end of the outdoor court. They collided under the netless rims, guessing where each other was going to be, throwing arms wide, gripping jerseys. The ball skipped low on the ground between them, hand to hand. Patete thought he would never be so long-armed, so teenaged, so sure of where his feet hit the ground. He watched Superchicken among them, shorter and pushing harder than the others, pointing and shouting, one hand in the air, the other loose and kinetic at his side. The ball stammered, started one way, got fearless, stopped; started another way, struck, marked time, started again; then seemed to have found a direction, struck again, got stuck.

And then Lil appeared, stepping out of the blue Honda before it roared toward home. Patete crouched in the bleachers, staring at her as she laughed and clapped – not at all the same person as the day before, when she bent double, holding her stomach, spitting and wiping spit away. Patete pressed his face against the metal bleacher, watching as Superchicken brought the ball up court from his baseline, passing close by Lil, not looking, then suddenly turned and pretended to throw the ball at her. She shrugged her shoulders in mock reflex, not even taking her hands out of her pockets. Her laugh rolled toward Patete across the court, across the grass, slowing to a stop where he sat, as if waiting to see what he would do next.

He hopped down, pocketing the candy, and peered out from behind the bleachers. Nobody was looking in his direction so he stood and hurried casually across the open space, facing away from the court. He heard dribbling in an unpredictable rhythm behind him. A silence, then a backboard shaking. He wondered what was happening, but he squinted into the low sky, seeing more spots than sun, not daring to look in their direction. The whole world seemed to be just behind him, out of sight, focused and sharp, magnetic. Lil laughed again and he knew he had missed something that was something to her. He wondered how many laughs he had missed in the months that had passed, and felt the first great pain of his life.

Finally he reached what he had seen – the long low racks, the bicycles neatly rowed, unchained. He recognized Superchicken's bike from the day before: an old Huffy scraped clean of bumper stickers, spraypainted purple, a bell twisted onto the spokes with a paperclip. He glanced at the basketball court; Superchicken was pretending to smack Lil's face, slapping the air. She slapped back at him and he clapped his hands together, the sound resonant and full, pretended to stagger backward.

"If I had fists and feet, I could hit and run," Patete whispered to himself, imagining himself attacking like a bird out of the bushes, unhuman and brutal. "And at least Lil would see me with a missing tooth or stitches, and a blacker eye. She would say, what were you thinking Patete? And I would say, don't call me that."

Instead he reached and, taking both handlebars, pulled the purple Huffy out of the rack. The grips were cold in his hands. He looked up and Lil was staring at him, shaking her head as, fast from behind her, Superchicken was sprinting toward him.

"Run, Patete, now,"
Lil shouted over the
sound of the wind
already rushing in
his ears.

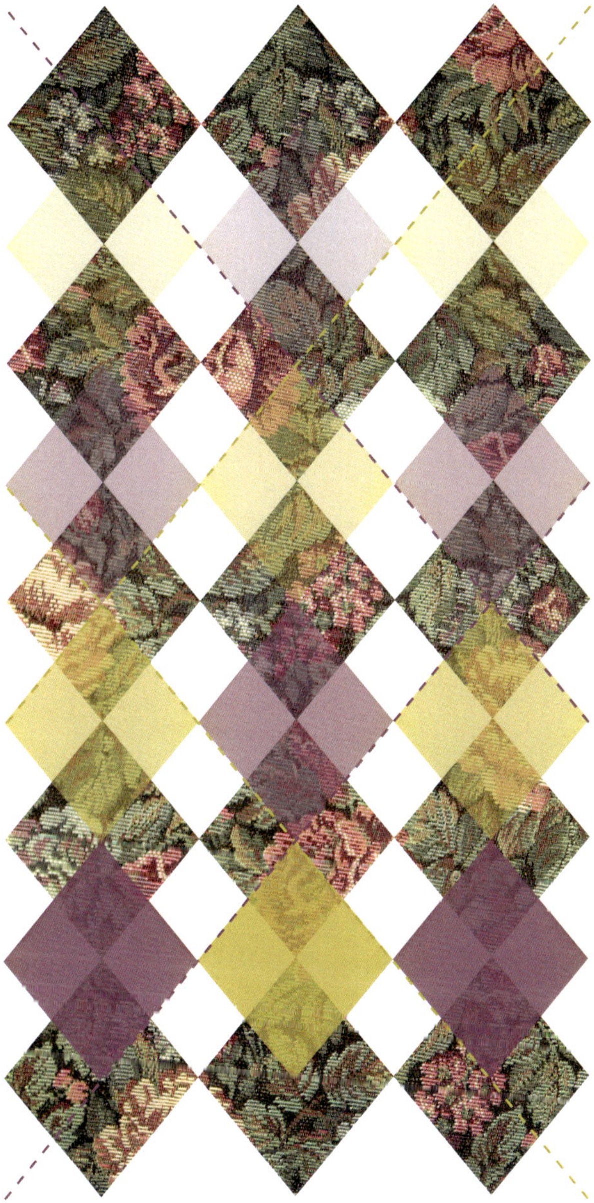

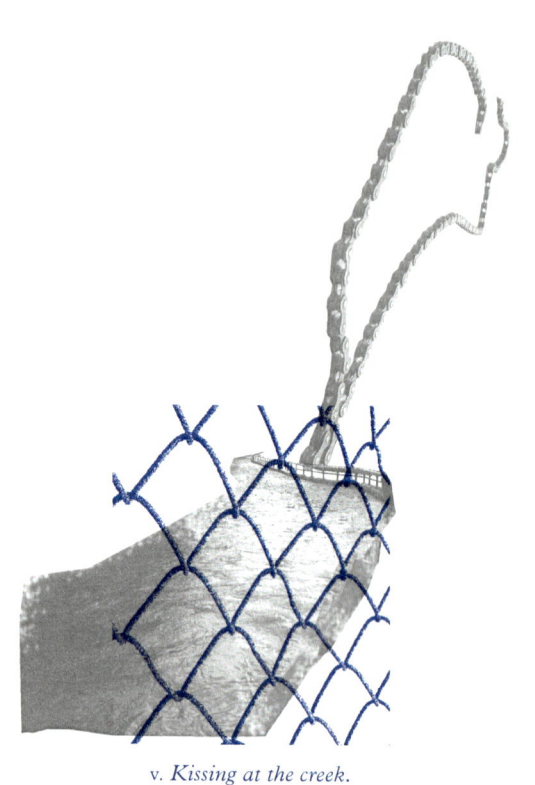

v. Kissing at the creek.

The very edge, the lip edge, was dirty and dipped down toward the water. Patete pedaled so hard that the seat creaked and the chain broke, gumming useless against the spinning tires. At the last moment he kicked the bicycle out from underneath his legs, hitting the ground and rolling as it bounced to the edge of the embankment, then tipped over and was gone. He stood, brushing his knees, and walked to the edge to see a misshapen circle spreading in the muddy water.

A car came barreling into the recycling lot, a hundred feet away. It was the blue Honda. She unlocked the doors. The driver's seat was as far forward as it could go. Patete ran around the car and opened the passenger door, sitting into her candy-wrapper smell.

"Boy you're in some trouble."

"I am?"

"You have to ask?" She cracked the window. "Quiet." But it was only a train on the tracks. "Don't you know what he's like? What were you thinking?"

"I thought maybe I'd sell it to Dom. I thought I could get some money, maybe buy something." He did not finish what he wanted to say.

"Oh Patete," she said and shifted into drive, kicked at the accelerator. "How much did he give you?"

"Dom said if it was stolen, he would beat me silly. A stolen bike at his door means cops at his door. So I ran it into the creek."

The engine thunked through the gears and they cut up an alley. Bricks slid past, weaving close on either side, then dropped away as the car soared without slowing across oncoming traffic. She tried to cut the steering wheel and nearly made it, might have made it except for a UPS truck parked at the corner. Her fender clipped the truck's back tire and it burst in thunder and rubber that flew like shrapnel, shattering the windshield in spidering grey-green cracks. The car fishtailed into the side of the truck and stopped dead. Patete had to crawl over the gearshift and out of Lil's door, after her.

"What the hell is that truck doing there, nine on a Saturday morning?

"You wrecked his car. What will he do when he sees it?"

"What? Who?" before she realized. "Don't worry, Patete," she said softly. "Maybe I can talk to him, maybe I can fix it."

She pulled at his arm, tugging him around the side of the building and Patete saw that they were standing in the schoolyard. The high metal fence was ten steps away. She pushed through it and he pushed through after her.

His arm was bleeding through his sweatshirt. He wished that she would notice, come and roll up the sleeve, but she was standing with her back to him, facing the house. Around her, the grass was tall on every side. The curling leaves, winter thin, waved in the morning air.

"I should go and tell him about his car," she said. "We should go around the house and come in the front door, make something up."

But instead she took his hand and led him deeper into the grass. When they could almost see the windows, but not quite, she stopped and was very still.

"Remember last summer, Patete, when we used to go swimming in the creek? I never told anybody about that."

"Why not?"

The grass was taller than Patete. He felt its razor edges on every side except where Lil's body parted it, in front of him. He felt like he had been swallowed by the fence, the grass, the yard.

"How old are you, Patete?"

"I'm still eleven."

"That makes me still thirteen. A lot can happen in a few months, Patete. Things that make you a different person."

"Okay," he said. "But you don't seem different to me."

She might have touched his hand; he wasn't sure. Around them, the wrinkle leaves on the stalks rippled together, like fragile fingers reaching for something ancient and certain.

"Maybe some things never change," she said. She turned to face him. His mouth was so close to hers that clouds of her wrapped his neck. "Look at me, Patete. When you look at me, I don't seem so different to me, either."

She came closer, blinking slowly, her eyes crossing slightly, as if she were hunting a reflection in Patete's wet eyes. When they met he closed his mouth into hers, not knowing how, only knowing why, and breathed her in as deep as he could.

Afterward, he said, "That's all there is to it?"

"That's all there is," she said. "I'm sorry." And they sat deep in the grass choosing candy out of his palm, biting the sugar shell away from the sour centers.

45

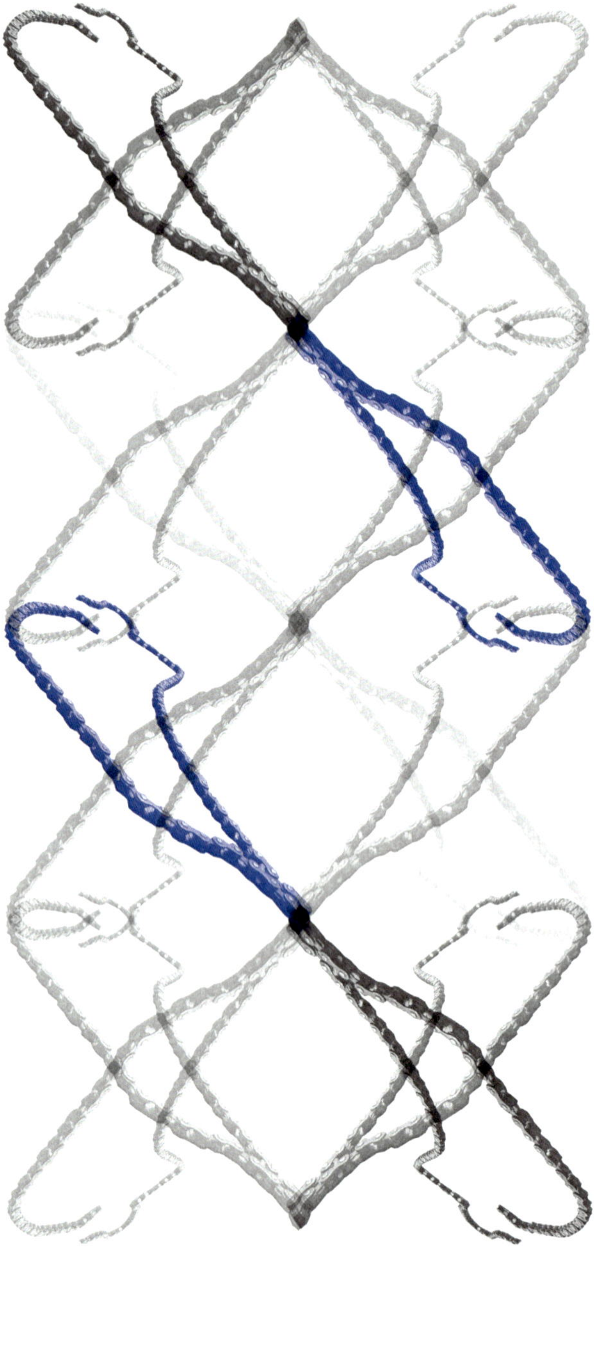

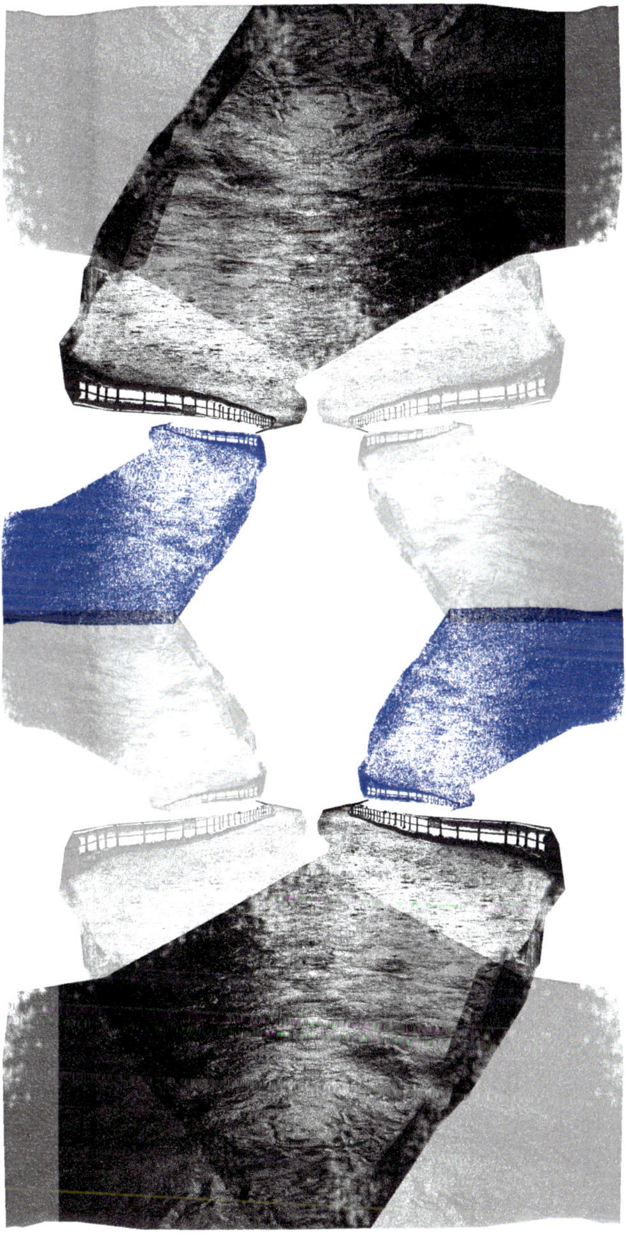

vi. *Lock and cock it.*

It was after noon when she woke to the sound of the doorbell. It rang over and over, fast, echoing itself. Balled hands pounded the door.

She got up slowly from the kitchen floor, both hands on her forehead. She felt her way through the house in the curtained dark, not turning lights on as she went. The front door was outlined in daylight; two shadow feet scuffed erratically on the boards of the porch.

"Momma, Mom, please just turn the knob, quick," she heard through the door. She pressed her eye to the view hole.

"Patete, what have you done now?" she called. His face filled the fisheye lens, streaked with tears. Behind him, a car she had never seen before pulled short at the edge of the yard. As its door opened a boy was already running out of it, his face shining with rage, his arms already stiffening.

Patete turned, saw, threw himself against the door once again, knowing it would not open. Shaking his head, his mouth gaped against the unyielding wood.

"No, Mom. Please."

The deadbolt tripped closed beneath her fingers, the steel filling the lock. And as she watched, he turned to face the yard. Other boys poured out of the car, forming a half circle, stomping, laughing.

"Someday you'll be a man," his mother called through the wood. "Be strong, Patete. Kick his ass."

Superchicken tore off his sweatshirt as he reached the steps, not slowing. Patete stepped out from beneath the shaded porch to meet him, his fists lifted small.

The Houses Under the Sea, the Dancers Under the Hill

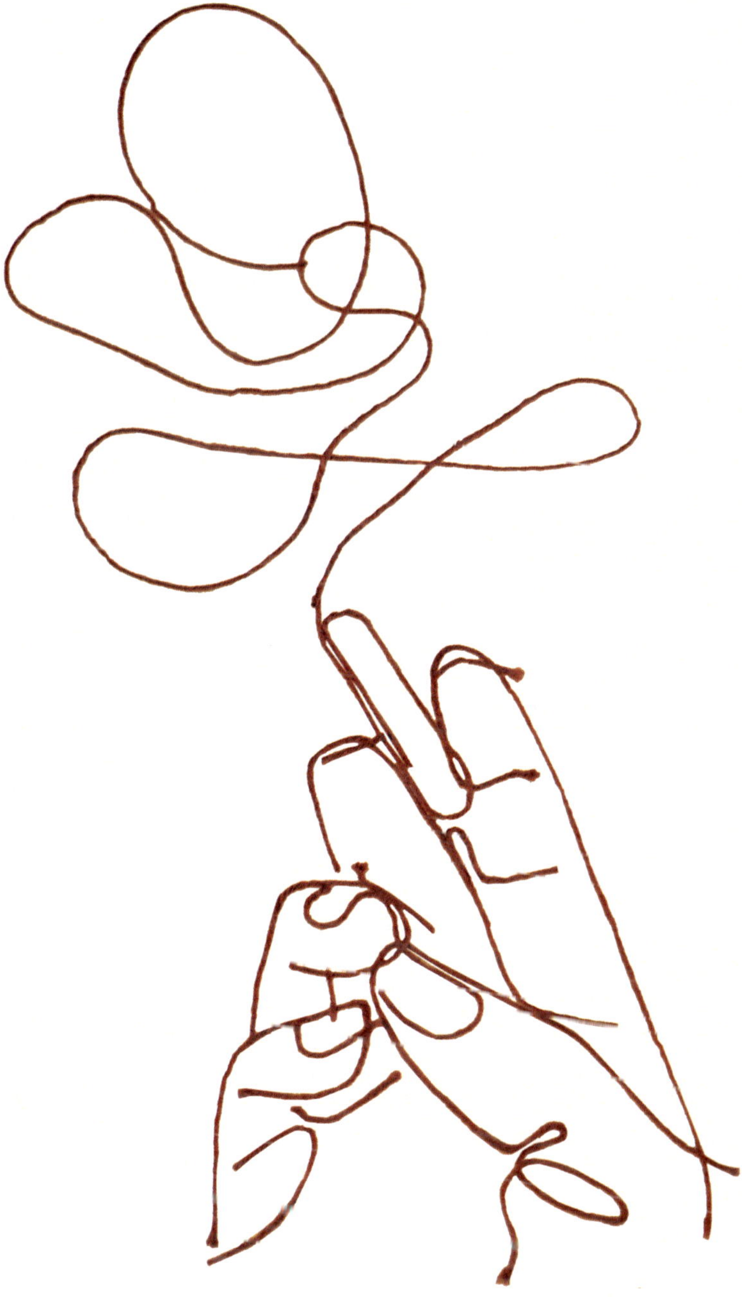

I.

Like most things that end, Tate's job ended simply. He was seated at the greeter's station, stamping museum passes for a student group, when a shoplifter sprinted from the gift shop. Tate strained up in his seat to shout after the boy, who looked back to laugh—slow old man—and didn't see the plate glass window. He must have thought it was a wide open, clean escape, still running even as his body crumpled in mid-stride, bunching upon itself and falling to the tile. The neat rows of students broke and swarmed around the boy as Tate shambled across the lobby, his hands trembling on his hips, and stood laughing until the museum guard arrived.

Within an hour, a video was posted on YouTube. Tate in his greeter's vest, stooped over the shoplifter and wagging a long finger in his face. The lens zoomed and Tate's fierce smile filled the screen, the big gums and little teeth, small and sharp as if he'd never lost his milkteeth; his chin doubled and the skin of his neck shaking, white whiskers invisible against his flushed and sweating skin.

"Like a stupid bird," Tate said over and over, his laugh echoing in the stone lobby, the audio slightly out of sync.

When he came back from lunch for his afternoon shift, he found the museum director waiting by the time clock. She showed him the video.

"You're wearing a museum vest, Tate," she said, rewinding and watching it again. "That's not how we treat visitors."

She pulled a scribbled pink slip out of her pocket. No fuss, no formalities; she only said, "Please leave your vest and badge at the ticket counter". Instead, Tate wadded them into a ball and pushed them into a trash can outside the employee entrance. Then he walked down the concrete steps toward the courthouse. He wanted to see Bailey, to tell her what had happened, how the kid got what he deserved, how there was a video on the Internet to prove it.

But across High Street, there was a crowd of gawkers gathered to watch the blue flashing lights that circled the courthouse. People rummaged in pockets, to snap photos with their cell phones. Tate pulled out his phone, too, and pushed redial.

"It's okay, Dad, we evacuated a few minutes ago," Bailey said when she answered. "Some idiot snuck a gun past security and waved it around one of the courtrooms like an idiot, like a hero. Swearing that he'd kill someone, then himself, unless he was allowed a clear line of fire at the defendant."

"Don't tell me that. What father wants to hear that?"

"It's over now," she said. "But the Mayor is already in front of the news cameras, promising new high tech screeners. So we're loading everything onto trucks and carting it all down to the Choo Choo hotel. Turning conference rooms into makeshift courtrooms."

He pictured Bailey somewhere in the crowd ahead of him, facing sirens and TV microphones with the other judges, her head poking out of the black polyester accordion folds of the robes. Directing crews as they loaded witness stands onto flatbed trucks.

"I'm having a bad day, too, Bailey. I got fired." He said it as half-confession, half-plea, a family ritual.

"I heard," she said gently. "It doesn't matter. And anyway the timing is perfect, because the City will be looking for security temps. You can keep me company."

So as Tate climbed the ridged metal stairs onto a city bus, he was glad he got fired; he had taken the job, after all, to be closer to the courthouse. As the bus swung under stoplights and brushed overhanging tree limbs, he thought about that day, six months before, when Judge Bluford had designated Bailey as his *pro tem*. Bluford was dying of cancer and said he'd be damned before he let a grey-haired pack of white wolves tell him whom he could, or could not, appoint to wear his robes. That it had done them good to call him, a black man, Sir. And it was high time they did the same for a woman, even if she was white.

And so he appointed Bailey to sit in his place on the Bench. Bailey, who had never argued a criminal case, who had barely made partner in her firm, not even thirty years old.

"That's my Bailey," Tate had told the old Judge over the sound of the oxygen machine, "the only girl man enough for the job."

Bluford didn't reply, the tubes swinging slowly back and forth from his nostrils.

::

Tate's one-room apartment was at the far end of a cul-de-sac of homes, a few blocks over from the chicken plant. The houses were all built in the forties with fat footers and shake siding, deep porches and unruly rosemary bushes; but the original hand-waxed doors had been replaced with metal safety doors pressed to look like wood. Bailey had found the room for him, around the corner from the two-bedroom townhouse she rented. Inside his apartment, the cabinets were empty except for boxes of cereal and canned tuna with pop-top lids. The walls and shelves were a faint white, empty of framed photographs or paintings; the only color in each room was from layers of paint peeling around the door frames.

The following afternoon, when his watch clicked to four o'clock, Tate appeared in the fleur-de-lys foyer of Bailey's office with a bagged peanut butter sandwich in each hand. He waited for her by the elevator, and when she came downstairs they walked the four blocks down Main Street toward the sprawling hotel. Past the new loft housing; past tables set out in front of the bakery for sweet tea and microwave pastries, where secretaries talked all day about the God-it's-hot-if-you'll-excuse-my-language-summer-sun; past the Mr. Zip with its ferocious orange walls and green lettering over the gasoline pumps, its bins of bagged ice, its public pay phone with the receiver long since stolen. They turned into an alley and walked faster, hurrying out of the sun and into the shade of the of the hotel.

At the end of the loading docks there was a break in the wall, where the brown brick façade ended in a ragged edge of bare block. Set into the block was a short staircase of yellowed wood and a plywood door. Bailey unlocked its chain with a key from her pocket, stepping past trash bins and drains cut into the slab floor. She pulled the door closed after them, locked it, and then led Tate along the long rows of Pullman train cars that had been parked in the hotel's gravel yard for nearly four decades – wired and piped into permanent hotel suites. Tate could hear families behind the window blinds, watching pay-per view movies or toweling off from the swimming pool.

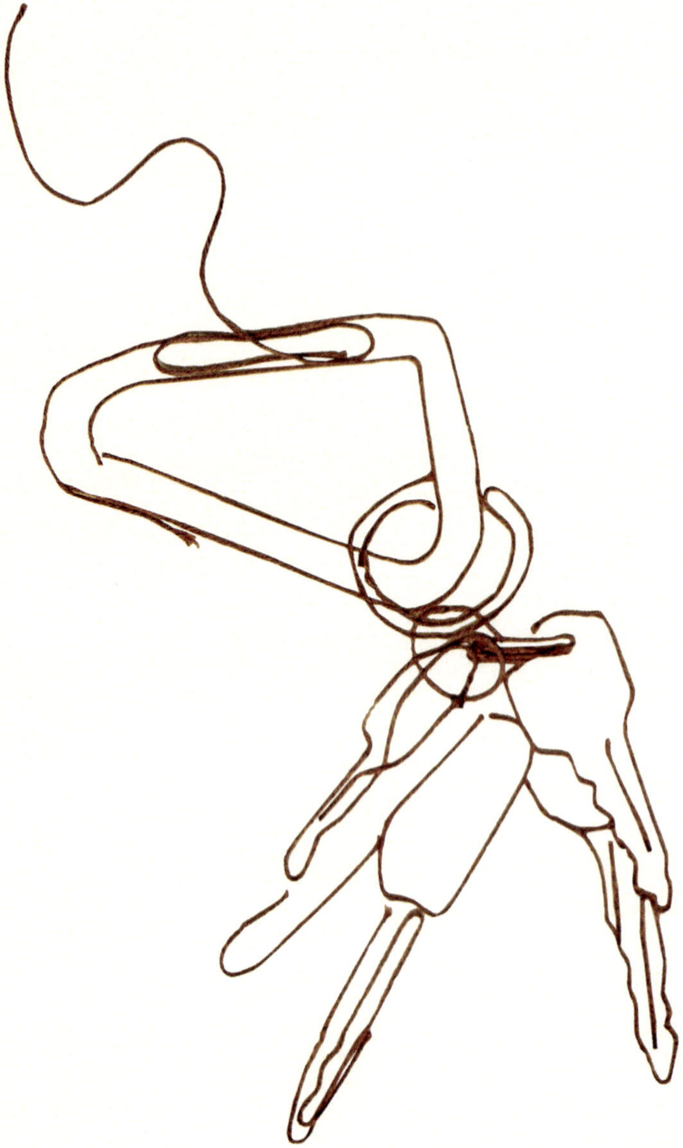

"Your mother and I stayed here on our honeymoon," he said. "It cost a hundred fifty dollars a night, and that was back in 1976."

"Wow, Dad. I guess you don't go on a honeymoon every day," she said, as if she'd never heard it before.

Suddenly a man's voice shouted from behind them. "Hey you two. You're not supposed to be here."

They turned to see a bailiff in a brown uniform hurrying toward them. Bailey waved.

"Oh, it's you, Judge," the man said. "I didn't know you out of your robes." He took off his hat and the sun hit his thick, pale, clean-shaven face. His eyes were heavy blue, matching the uniform. "I haven't had a chance to talk to you, since yesterday," he said. "But I'm glad to get a minute. I'm sorry as hell about what happened."

"It's over now," Bailey said.

"Not to me, Judge. I nearly resigned this morning."

"You can't do that, Ronald. Who would keep us safe?" As Tate watched, she reached out and touched the man on his arm, above the sweating crease of his elbow. "I'd like to introduce my father."

The bailiff squeezed Tate's hand, too earnestly. "You should be real proud."

"Of Bailey?" Tate said, and the bailiff grinned to hear her name spoken informally, like he was being let in on a secret.

"Dad's one of our temp security guards."

THE HOUSES UNDER THE SEA, THE DANCERS UNDER THE HILL   57

The bailiff led them along the wall to a service entrance and, from a closet inside the door, brought out a blue baseball cap with the Choo Choo logo screenprinted across the crown. He tucked a handheld radio into the cap and passed it to Tate.

"What about keys?" Tate asked.

"You won't need them," the bailiff said. "Just keep the walkie-talkie on, and let us know if you see anything out of the ordinary."

"And what does ordinary look like?"

"Don't be smart, Dad. You'll figure it out," Bailey said, heading down the hall. Tate followed her, tracing the intricate carpet patterns with the toe of his shoe as he walked.

"You know why they make these designs so fancy?" he said to Bailey's back. "The more elaborate the patterns the better they hide dirt."

"They're pretty, too," Bailey said.

She cracked the door to a conference room so Tate could peek in. He saw the jury box and witness stand set into place, families already starting to fill in rows of folding metal chairs.

"It took all night and all morning to set up," Bailey said. "We should have waited until tomorrow to reopen testimony, but City Hall insisted. Too many news anchors asking if justice is sitting on her hands."

The next door along the corridor opened onto a hotel suite. The beds had been removed and Judge Bluford's battered oak desk was set up in their place. Bailey pulled two chairs to the front of the desk and set out the sandwiches.

"Why don't you ever sit in the Judge's chair?"

"Doesn't feel right," she said. "It's not mine to sit in."

"The Bench isn't yours, either."

"Come on, Dad, you know better than that," she said, sucking peanut butter off her teeth. "The Bench doesn't belong to any one person."

Tate watched her flip through notes from the day before, her mouth moving as she read. He walked the small suite, his eyes touching her business cards stacked on the corner of the desk, the box of manila folders with her name scrawled in marker. He counted moths like folds of paper in the window sill. Bailey's chair squeaked on its hinges as she leaned forward, a tiny sound perfectly in tune with the muted coughs and voices filtering in from the room next door.

"This case is a nightmare," she said. "For me, it can't finish fast enough."

"It'll end when you end it."

"I wish it were that easy," she shrugged. "And anyway, I've got no business presiding over a jury. I was only supposed to hear civil cases; I only said yes to this one because the docket was full. But right now I'd give anything for a sweet, simple divorce case."

"Don't be cynical, Bailey," Tate muttered. "It's cheap."

"You think so, Dad?" she said, hand-cranking the window open, fanning herself. "When everything went crazy yesterday, when that man showed up with his gun and everyone lost their mind, there was a seven year old girl on the stand."

"The man with a gun was in your courtroom? You never told me that."

"She'll be back up there today," Bailey said, ignoring him. "Trying to put words together, but too young to understand what she's supposed to say. I know what she means, everyone does. But it's my job to get it on record. So I let the lawyers ask her over and over, horrible questions. And every time she points at the defendant, she doesn't point at his face. She points lower, lower, while the smirk on his face grows, like he doesn't care who sees." She sipped coffee from a mug, her back to him. "And you say cynicism is cheap?"

"It's not your job to get it on record, Bailey. It's your job to fix it. To fix him."

Tate knew all the testimony, the motions and countermotions, because Bailey told him the details of each case at the end of the day. Sitting on the porch of his apartment building, he had heard the intimacies of dozens of divorces, of children split between houses and holidays. Blow by blow, fracture by fracture, families coming apart as lovers and parents wound intricate webs of half-truths and half-lies through the courtroom. Bailey would tell how she had tried carefully to unwind them, without breaking a single strand, to minimize the pits and pieces of themselves that they would carry, sticking to them, out into the world.

So he had heard all about the allegations against a rich kid from the Bluffs. Sipping Starbucks while she talked, his mind had wandered to sunny Sundays when Bailey was young, how he used to take her joyriding there, up the two-lane road to the subdivisions overlooking the city. Among the new construction houses dotting the woods, he would make a show of writing down telephone numbers off realtors' signs. Seeing his little sedan reflected in the wide expanses of windows, he would tell Bailey to wave, pretending that her reflection waved back from inside the house.

But last night had been different. Returning from the police station in the early afternoon, she had been silent, not wanting to talk about the case. Instead, she asked Tate to come home with her, to sit up and read with her, in the living room of her townhouse. She lay tucked onto a half-sofa with her stocking feet on the armrest; whenever he trailed off, she had shaken him awake, pulling from a stack of French detective novels, translations of Simenon opened to her favorite chapters. The stories were perfect, she said, for anyone fiddling with the law – reminders not only of *homo praesumitur*, but also that, at heart, anyone is capable of anything.

"She's only seven years old, for God's sake." Her voice caught. "Do you remember when I was seven? I get the years mixed up."

Tate shuffled through memories like photos jumbled out of a cardboard box. Bailey newborn in the incubator, safe beneath the hard plexiglass shell. Holding tight to her as he changed diapers, bathed her, lifted her into the crib, squeezing her leg hard not to drop her. But it was the day of her seventh birthday that he remembered

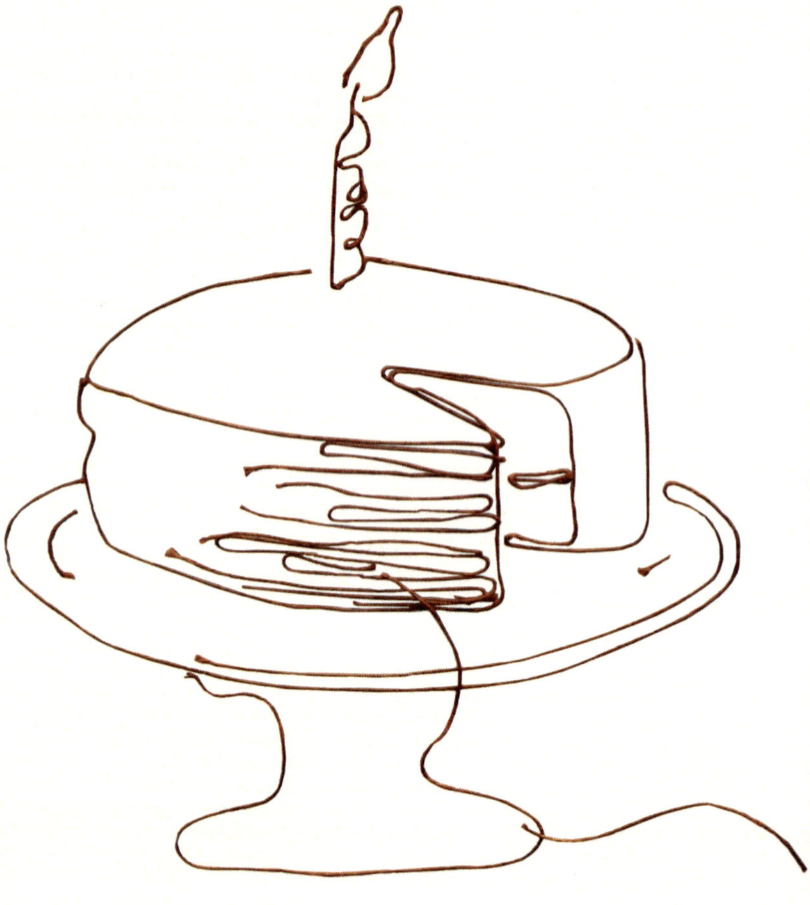

in perfect, unbending detail, the night her mother emptied half their bedroom into suitcases and was gone. The birthday morning, a cake was baked by an aunt, gifts were bought at the drugstore and hurriedly wrapped by neighbors. Standing against the wall while the others sang, Tate had scratched at his stomach. As Bailey blew out her candles, searching around for smiles, he had slipped out of the room to pull off his shirt in the bathroom mirror, tracing the spread of chicken pox that snaked around his middle and up his chest. By nightfall, his body was covered.

The doctor had prescribed Tylenol and quarantine, but as he sweated and cursed in the silent room, his body smeared in egg yolk and linseed oil, he had a realization. He crept down the hall, quiet not to wake her, and into her bedroom; knelt slowly, ceremoniously, beside her bed and buried his face in her pillow, resting his seeping pores against her soft cheek. Within a week she was covered in a rash that matched his own, feverish under the gaping scabs. But two weeks later, she was safe forever. The innocent infected, and so inoculated.

For Tate, this changed everything. The first day Bailey was recovered enough to go outside, he borrowed a canoe and took her out on the river. She laughed and splashed backward at him, delighting in the sun until the river tipped, her face first confused then terrified as he rocked the boat back and forth until it flipped, her breath going high in her chest then pinching off in the cold water.

"Sink or swim," he shouted when he reached the bank.

A week later, he put her in the front seat of the car. Out of the booster seat for the first time, allowed to sit up front with him, she grinning until he sped the curves of a dark country road, headlights off, and she clutched the dashboard and whispered for him to stop. When she had a nightmare of dogs nipping at her heels, Tate searched the highway until he found a mound of fur and flesh at the side of the road, taking her hand in his in the headlights and stretching it out to touch the putrid remains, then handing her a shovel from the trunk to bury it.

"You'll never be scared of dogs again," he said as she dug, the dirt at her feet flecked salt wet.

Now, as she stood at the window, he told her: "Sit down, Bailey, and finish your coffee."

"You know what I might do instead?" she asked. "I might take that box of case files off the desk and pour it out the window. Let anyone read them, anyone who will; let them tell me what I should do."

"I already told you what to do," he said but she looked past him, at the hotel alarm clock still ticking seconds from the bedside table.

"I should go," she said, reaching into the mirrored closet for the long black judge's robes.

::

Tate pulled the Choo Choo cap down on his head and twisted the dial on the handheld radio. He walked Building Two, his assigned beat, for an hour, two hours, he wasn't sure. The carpets all looked alike – the same patterns repeated around every corner, the same threadbare wear and tear showing at every entrance. He counted hotel room doors as he passed them, lost count, circled back and started over. At last he pushed through an unmarked exit and found himself at the long string of Pullman suites, the plywood door and its squat yellow stairs. Propping the door open, he sat down. The sun poured, thick as rain, down the back of his neck.

The alley was framed with dumpsters and stacks of shipping pallets under the angled canopies of barbed wire that guarded gravel lots. In one of the lots were row after row of port-a-potties, ready for rental – a constant target for kids in the neighborhood. They would come from blocks around, carrying matted blankets stolen from yard sales or dumpsters. One would sit onto another's shoulders and drape the blankets, triple-folded, over the barbed wire so they could scramble up and over the chain-link fence, already unwrapping the plastic from enormous fireworks. To laugh the next morning as they walked to school, pointing at the plastic doors knocked off their hinges, the spattered explosions that colored the insides of the port-a-potties brown and fanned out ten feet across the ground.

Tate's forehead was wet under the sweatband of the cap. The afternoon's late heat pushed down on the city like a sweaty palm, the street rising in hazy waves to meet it. Through the door behind him, he could see into the hotel's flower garden. Shadows of canvas awnings cut across disheveled parents drowsing in teak lounge chairs, and strobed children as they ran up and down the sidewalk, yelling. Goldfish fluttered from shade to shade in the lily pond. On the far side of the garden, a woman stood in the brunt of the sun, striking one match after another, letting each flare and burn without lighting the cigarette that angled out of her mouth. She was younger than Tate by ten years, but her face had a worn look and her body was shapeless inside her clothes. As Tate watched, she stepped quickly along the sidewalk and, looking left and right, backed through the open door of a Pullman car.

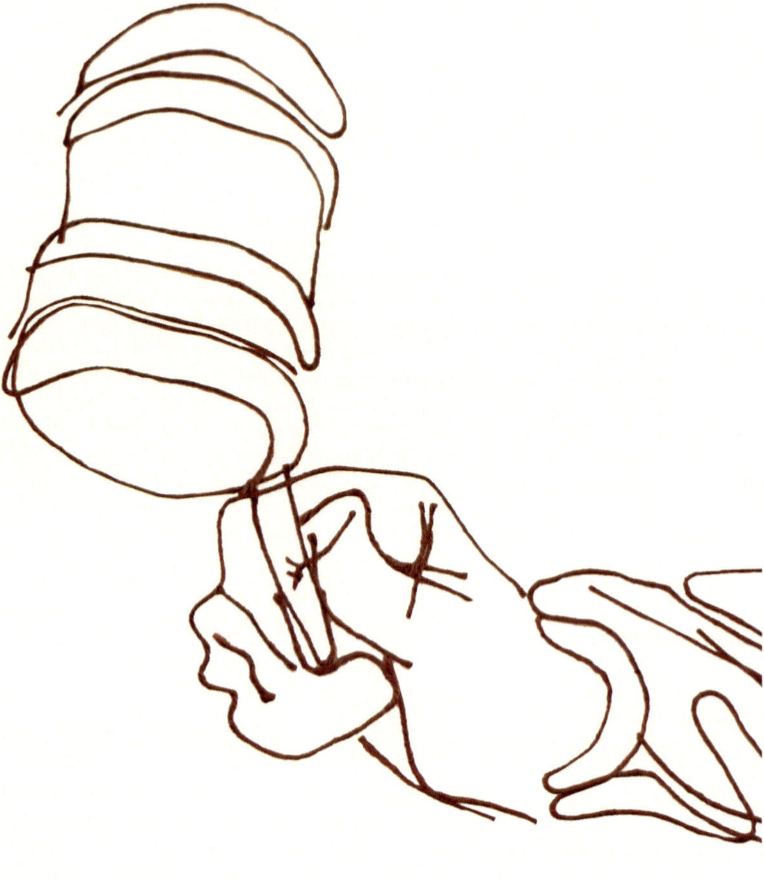

Tate wrapped both hands around the radio, as if he were warming his hands by its battery. But instead of pressing the call button, he crossed to the suite and stepped through the door after her.

Inside, the train car was like any other hotel room, with open Venetian blinds and sunlight striping the unmade bed, clothes rumpled on the floor. The woman bent over an open suitcase, a dozen twenty dollar bills in her hand.

"Hey lady," Tate said, sharpening his voice. "You supposed to be in here?"

The woman looked at his blue cap with its chugging train logo bearing down on her. She folded the money, a reflex.

"I can explain."

Tate held up the walkie-talkie.

"Okay, so maybe I can't," she said, then added without hesitation: "But if you haven't used that radio yet, maybe we can work something out." She lay two of the twenties on the open lid of the suitcase.

"I think we should step outside."

"It's better to talk here. Too many cops and courtrooms."

"I know. My daughter's a judge."

"Oh is she?" the woman said. "Isn't that just my luck?"

Tate went out of the room first and stood waiting. For a moment he thought the woman might gather her skirt and run past him down the sidewalk, but she only sat onto the wall of a flower bed, arranging pleats around her lap. She pulled a tattered pack of cigarettes from a hidden pocket and lit one. The glow instantly clouded over with ash.

"Your daughter is the lady judge?"

"She's not a real judge, she's filling in for a sick man. But he chose her out of every lawyer in the city."

"She seems real enough from where I sit," the woman said. "You should be proud."

"I keep hearing that," he said.

The woman watched Tate. Her cheeks hollowed around the cigarette's filter, like it was sucking back.

"Brave and smart, both. She must get that from you, mister. You a judge, too?"

"I just told you, she's not a real judge."

"Oh right," she exhaled fast, stumbling for the right words. "I couldn't ever do that job, it doesn't come natural to me. That's why I always avoided the jury duty, until now."

"You're a juror? Did you return a verdict?"

"Not yet. We're in deliberations."

Tate's hand went to the radio. "Aren't you sequestered?"

"No, it's okay. The bailiff wouldn't let me smoke inside." For several minutes she sat without speaking, then shifted to face him. "Look at me, mister. You know how I make my living?"

Tate looked at her unpainted nails, the hands smooth as pink plastic except for the two flaking and ochred knuckles where the cigarette butt nestled. Her hair was pulled back with a brown rubber band, every strand slicked so tightly that Tate thought if the rubber band broke loose, not one hair would shift out of place. He didn't want to guess.

"Well?" she demanded flicking the cigarette expertly with her forefinger.

"Waitress," he said, the first thing he could think of.

"In a restaurant? My wrists wouldn't hold up, though I've traded my knees for them. See here." She twitched up the long hem of her skirt. Her knees were callused white, the skin rough, as if it were dusted with coarse powder. "I clean houses. Used to have five of them up on the Bluffs."

"People let you in their homes?" he said roughly. "You always rummage through their luggage?"

"Fair enough, you've got me there," she said, chuckling. "But look, mister, I'm trying real hard here. Are you going to call the cops or what?" As he watched, she shook the pack and lit another. "Hold on. If your daughter's the judge, I might be able to help her. Or help you help her," she said. "I know things about the boy on trial in there, things I never told a soul."

"You aren't supposed to discuss the case," Tate said, not wanting her to stop. Thinking of how he could sit on the porch with Bailey, dropping hints until she asked him to tell her everything.

"Just think of me as a character witness," the woman said. "I used to clean his parents' house, years ago, back when he was a boy. He would sneak around after me, making messes where I'd just been. If his mother sent him outside, he'd hide in the bushes and throw rocks at my car. Not big ones, just big enough to scratch the wax. When I caught him at it, he asked why it mattered, since the car was so scratched already."

She looked down at her hands, not speaking for a moment, as if she held the things she was going to say cupped inside of them.

"They had a Christmas party once, for his class from school. It was his idea and his mother was so proud of him for being thoughtful. But I knew better. So I told her I could stay late, pass out cupcakes and clean up, and after all the games and popcorn what do you think I heard but one of the girls telling the boys that she'd show them something out back of the shed. She did it, too. I could see from the upstairs window as she dropped her shorts and the boys pointed, snickering and scared. Then out of nowhere comes a kid swinging a yellow whiffle ball bat, and smacks her right across the backside. He hit her good, too. I could see the color coming up on her thigh."

She paused for effect, framed by the flower bed. Tate sat waiting, knee to knee with her.

"I rushed downstairs to march the boy with the bat into the corner, but he was already there. Huddled in the kitchen corner with the favored son, who was counting dollar bills, one by one, into his hand. The kid with the bat walked away, and then, would you believe, guess who came in through the back door? That girl, with one hand pressed against the red welt on her leg and the other outstretched. Her eyes dripping anger and hurt and shame, but there to collect. Brave, like a soldier. But what do you think the little bastard did? He tossed the bills onto the floor, pointing and laughing as she bent to pick them up. I ran forward and held him against the wall, but he only laughed harder, saying it's fun to watch girls cry, asking if I was going to cry, too."

She inhaled smoke like it was cool water, her head back, and crushed the cigarette against her shoe.

"That's why I didn't skip out on jury duty this time, mister. The minute I saw he got arrested, and for what, I started praying I'd get a summons. And the minute I sat down in the juror's box, I started praying that he would glance in my direction, and recognize me, and remember. Take that grin he was born with and wipe it right off his face."

She stood stiffly, with effort, specks of ash falling from her fingers to twist, invisible, to the sidewalk.

"You've seen them houses, shining gold as the sunrise. Everybody wants a house like that. But can they live there without thinking they deserve to? Without thinking they deserve whatever they want. Once upon a time I was afraid of them, that they'd catch me doing something I shouldn't and I'd be out on my backside. But then I understood: they don't even see me, don't even notice I'm there. So maybe I should make them notice."

As the sky broke into evening, the hotel's first shift workers were leaving through doors set into the back wall, walking up the alley away from them. At the heavy traffic of Main Street they crossed from work to home, climbing over knee walls or sitting down at bus stops. One man stopped to rinse his face in a bird bath before disappearing around the corner.

"Holy Lord God," she said, eyes upward, "that little girl face and those soggy eyes and any fool can see that she's not fit to answer such questions. You tell your daughter the judge to make it stop. Tell her I know he hurt that little girl, I just know it. That it's okay for her to hate him, just a little bit. It's okay for her to hurt him back."

Tate stood after her.

"Bailey will fix it," he said.

The woman stamped her foot. "No, she hasn't got it in her."

Tate stepped toward her, speaking tenderly, almost as if to comfort her, almost to himself.

"You're wrong, lady. She's not scared. Just earlier today, I told her to fix him. To fix him good."

"Well, you better tell her again."

Tate had left the plywood door propped open, and through it he could see the dim outlines of the near Appalachians. Overhead, a small, irregular object – plane or bird or planet – wound its shadow up the street.

"After she turned seven, I had to be father and mother to Bailey," Tate said. "I remember standing for hours, listening to her breathing through her bedroom door, wondering how I was going to teach her everything I knew and everything I didn't know, too. I would watch her sleeping, peaceful, and think that children must have some clarity, some understanding that escapes us once we're grown. Some secret good that they know, only they don't know how to say it. But that all changed with the chicken pox."

He glanced at the woman, but she was fishing in the cigarette pack with her finger.

"One night, when her fever was at its worst, she wouldn't lay still. I went into the bedroom and she had kicked the sheets off her bed, and her legs were shaking like she was pretending to dance. I told her to stop, but she said she couldn't, looking up at me, her face sorry, saying she didn't understand. I carried her out to the bus stop, to the hospital, her forehead hot against my cheek. Thinking for the first time that there isn't something good and pure that children know. There's a fear-shaped hole in their minds, in their hearts, waiting for life to fill it up."

As Tate talked his face tightened, the old man skin shrinking around his teeth. He spoke slowly, testing every word, chewing to make sure it was solid before he spoke it.

"I spent five years teaching her all I could. And the day she turned twelve, I sent her to boarding school. Made sure she got on the Greyhound safe, and then cut her off. I wouldn't reply to her letters, I didn't answer when she called. Once, I picked up the phone by mistake and had to pretend it was a wrong number, saying, Hello? Who's there? before I hung up."

The woman whistled between her teeth.

"But she panicked. Ran away from school, bought a bus ticket home and jerked open the kitchen door. Grabbed the front of my shirt, asking why, what's the matter with you, but I would only tell her what she should have already learned, what I'd tried to teach her. That the lucky daughter, the beloved daughter learns two things – first, that she can trust her daddy to take care of everything. Second, that she can't."

"Hold on a minute," the woman said. "That isn't love."

Tate looked at the woman; she was bent forward, wadding the empty pack in her hands. She looked up, saw him staring.

"The hell it isn't," he said.

"It's not hard, mister. If it smells like love, it's love. If it doesn't, it's something else, maybe something better. You wanted to make her strong."

"And it worked. Look at her — Judge Bluford said she's the only girl in all of Chattanooga, man enough to sit the Bench."

"Sure it worked. All I'm saying is, sometimes you've got to choose between being good and being right. And if you want them strong, you've got to give them something to hate."

"Make her hate me, my own daughter? Don't you see that can't be true?" but he felt the bones of his face give way, his mouth going slack around the words, thinking: that's it, exactly.

The woman dropped the empty pack onto the sidewalk.

"Look here, I'm out of smokes. I should get inside before I get in trouble." She stifled a yawn. "I know what you're thinking, that stealing is a sin. But there's sin, and there's stupid. If a person leaves their hotel room door open, they turn it into a welcome mat."

"Just go," Tate said, in a voice without breath behind it.

THE HOUSES UNDER THE SEA, THE DANCERS UNDER THE HILL

"Okay, but there's one more thing," the woman said, already moving toward the door of the suite. "If you don't want those two twenties, I could put them to use."

She slipped back into the Pullman and Tate looked around him, his eyes groping through the garden, searching for the noisy tools in the distant swimming pool, buzzing insects in the garden, trucks out in the street. Anything not to see Bailey's face at twelve years old, her eyes dark with tears. Not to remember twisting her face away from himself, pushing her toward the kitchen sink as she vomited.

The woman came out of the train car with her hands in her pockets, just as the bailiff appeared around the corner.

"Where have you been?" he asked harshly, his wide pasty mouth almost shouting. "I've been looking everywhere."

"You said no smoking inside."

"I meant don't smoke. I didn't mean for you to sneak off."

"Nobody's sneaking," she muttered and followed him around the corner. Tate followed too, a few steps back, and waited outside Bailey's makeshift Chambers. After ten minutes, the bailiff came out, alone.

"All I said was there's no smoking in the building," he told

Tate. "Why couldn't she duck into the washroom like everybody else? You remember that, sir. You remember it to your daughter."

Half an hour later, Bailey declared a mistrial. She came into the hallway with the robe already draped over her arm.

"Dammit, Dad. What were you thinking?"

"This is my fault?"

"You're my father. I got you this job. When you shit, it splashes my shoes."

"You can't talk to me like that, Bailey," he said, snapping his fingers and pointing at her. "No matter how old you get, you'll always be my child."

"Your daughter," she said. "There's a difference." She handed the judge's robe to the bailiff, who held the door open without looking up. "Let's go, Dad. No sense staying here."

They walked the hallways and the gravel yard. When they reached the plywood door leading onto the yellow stairs, it was still propped open.

"Don't blame me, nobody gave me a key," Tate said, but Bailey pretended she hadn't heard.

The alley was deserted again, stretching soundless from their footsteps to the cars that sped Main Street. Bailey thought jealously of the first shift hotel workers, already in bed or slumped in front of televisions, not still facing a long walk home. She could hear her father muttering under his breath, watching as he repeated words over and over to himself, folding the air with an open hand. The leaves of a lone tree, planted in the sidewalk by the city, hissed in the breeze. Tate repeated himself louder, then louder again.

"Speak up, Dad."

"I say, you call that justice? You had a job to do."

"I did my job," she said. "That woman was out of sequester for fifteen minutes. It's unfair, by law."

"So he goes free. Is that fair?"

"I don't know. For now, anyway." Her voice was paper thin. "If it were up to me, I don't know what I would do to him. Maybe something awful."

"It was up to you, Bailey. You should have stayed strong."

She squinted down the street past him. The sun was setting at her back, shining red on his face.

"That's me," she said. "Your strong girl. The beloved girl."

"Don't you put that on me," he said, swallowing the words as he spoke them.

She shaded her eyes to see him; he was so close to her that her elbow touched his shoulder.

"Dad, do you remember when I was a kid and you would fall asleep in the hallway outside my room? I would crawl out beside you to watch you, and I would try to fall asleep on the floor beside you, but I never could. I was too excited, my face against your sleeve, the tips of my fingers on your arm, watching your breath slow down to nearly nothing. You seemed so strong to me, then, and I remember thinking that if I could just watch close enough, I might be able to share it."

She reached to touch him, feeling that her hand was very small against his arm, but he pulled away in a complicated shuffle, backing against the chain link fence. On the street behind them, a car slowed, and she turned around.

The car was the color of wet brass, wide and close to the ground, with twin grills flared like nostrils. It braked to a stop, engine idling. The driver's door opened and a man stepped out, tall, with a wide face behind thin-rimmed metal glasses. His sleeves were rolled high above broad hands; his tie was like a hammock, a loose smile.

"Judge? That you?"

The man held out his hand. Bailey hesitated, then took it.

"We thought it was you," he said. "We wanted to stop and tell you personally how pleased we are."

Bailey held on to the man's hand, pumping it up and down as if she couldn't let go.

"Son, come on out and thank the lady judge."

Bailey protested, but the boy unfolded out of the back seat of the car – black shoes and legs splayed wide, then the long torso and face, the carefully tousled hair. He's just a college kid, Tate thought. But he was taller than Bailey and as he looked down at her his eyebrows met his nose in deep shadow, the eyes beneath like watching mouths, red rimmed and hungry.

"God bless you, Judge," he said, his lips wet on the words.

"It wasn't my choice," Bailey said, looking at the boy's father. "A juror was out of sequester. It's the law."

"Whatever you say," the father told her. "But by our count, that's twice in two days."

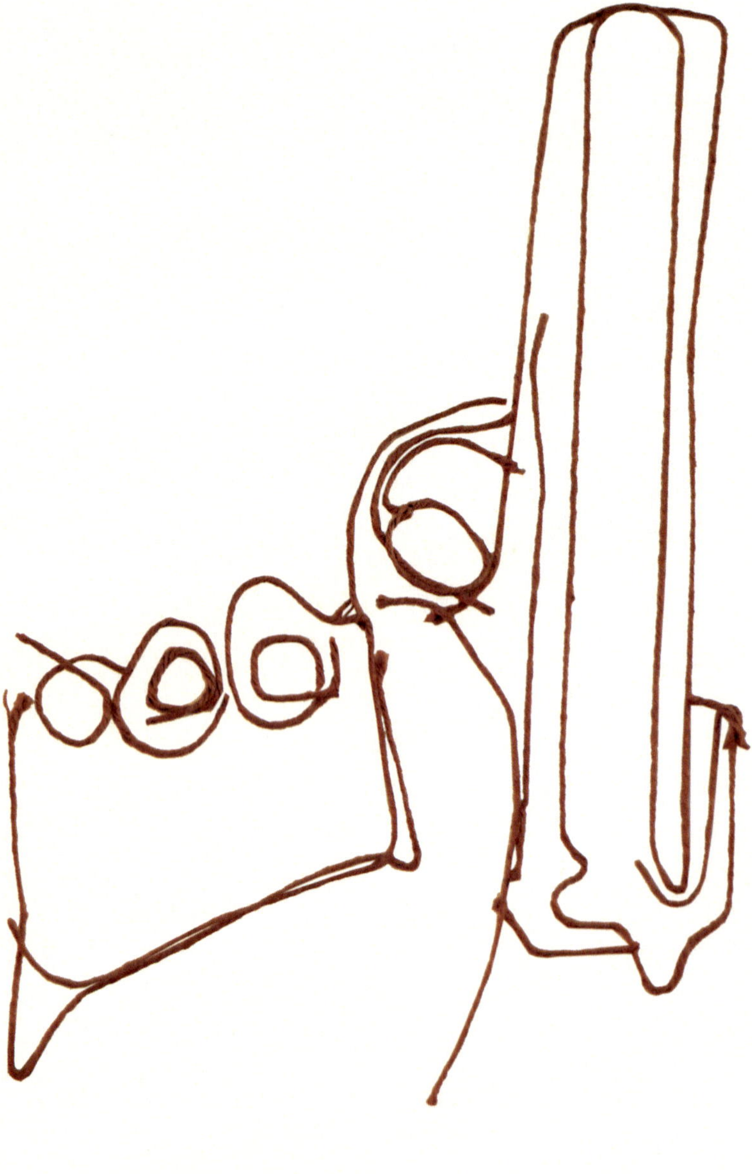

Tate pushed against Bailey, trying to take the man's hand. But she leaned backward, pressing him into the fence.

"Now, Bailey," Tate said roughly. "How about you let your old man out from behind your skirts?"

The man laughed. "The way we see it, that's not a bad place to be." His son looked at him, sudden and angry, and he laughed again.

A woman's voice came from inside the car, begging. "Can't we please go? I can't stay here another moment."

The man winked at Tate. "If Momma's not happy," he said, and put his hand onto his son's head, angling him into the back seat. The car pulled ahead and away, the boy's hand waving from the back window. Bailey let her hand drop. Overhead, the streetlights crackled on, their first light dropping to flare and fade.

"What did he mean, twice in two days?"

She shook her head. "I don't think you'd understand."

"Don't be ridiculous. I'm your father."

He wriggled out from between the fence and her shoulder, and they moved on through the blue wash of dusk. Tate hunched his collar together, thinking that he should get home before the air turned cold. But as they turned the corner, he saw the shining brassy car parked beneath the high rain roof of Mr. Zip, and the three of them — father, boy, mother — inside at the counter.

Bailey hung back, protesting, but Tate went inside. He crossed the store to the refrigerator shelves set into the far wall, pulled open a glass door and watched through it.

The man was arguing loudly with the clerk, demanding to know why the store didn't stock champagne.

Tate picked up a cardboard six-pack of beer and walked up the center aisle toward the register. As he came closer, the boy's mother rounded into view, holding a two-liter bottle of ginger ale and a carton of eggs. She wore a thick jacket, plush and textured, and her knee-length dress was an abstract pattern, shyly stylish. The fluorescent light slashed deep lines in the soft of her cheeks and shaded her hair with streaks of grey pencil. Wrinkles around her mouth were a maze of wandering paths, filled at the corners with dribbles of saliva that she didn't bother to wipe away.

"Hey, I know you," the clerk called out. "You're that woman on the news." Tate looked up to see him pointing at Bailey, who cringed in the doorway. "You're that lady judge."

"Sure, it's her," the boy's father said. "She's the reason we're looking for champagne. To toast her."

"And if she's the knight in shining armor, then you're the damsel in distress," the clerk said, pointing at the tall boy, the son, as he shrank backward against chips in glossy bags and yellow quarts of oil.

The clerk's round face grinned. "The both of you together, right here in the Mr. Zip. Can I take your picture? I want to post it on my Facebook."

Tate pushed forward to the counter, the six pack of beer cold in his hand. "Why are you calling her a knight in armor? She's no such thing."

"That man is her father," the tall man whispered to the clerk, winking and laughing. "I guess he's not impressed."

"For God's sake, impressed with what?" Tate pleaded.

"Didn't she tell you? And even if she didn't, how could you miss it? I thought old men watch the news."

Tate looked at Bailey, thinking of how she asked him to her apartment – read with me, she had said, stay up with me – until long after the six o'clock, ten o'clock, eleven o'clock broadcasts were over.

"Wait a minute, I've got a copy of the newspaper somewhere," the clerk said as Bailey came up the aisles to take Tate's arm, to tug him gently toward the door. He pushed her hand away. "It doesn't matter, I know it by heart. The whole city does. Man showed up in her courtroom with a gun, but nobody noticed. The guards were distracted and the lawyers were busy with their yellow pads, just like on TV. And before anybody realized, he was standing at the Bench, with a pistol in her face."

"Please Daddy, don't listen," Bailey whispered in Tate's ear.

"Everyone gasped. No, not the Judge. Only she isn't the Judge, is she? The paper said the real Judge is down at the hospital, sucking chemo from a plastic tube. Your daughter just happened to be sitting in his seat. Wrong place, wrong time."

Bailey stopped pulling at Tate and hid her face in her hands.

"They say he pushed the gun so hard against her forehead that it left a mark, and shouted that if everyone did what he said, he'd let her go. That he'd let everybody go except one, that he'd unload every bullet except one, because one is all it would take for him and his little girl to put this behind them forever. And you know what? Everybody did. They all took a step away from the poor defendant. From you," he said, pointing at the boy. "Nobody was going to do a thing to help you, nobody was going to lift a finger."

"I can't take this any more," said the wife's voice, the mother's voice, from behind Tate.

"You shut up," her husband told her.

"But not the Judge," said the clerk. "She stood up and came down from the Bench, across the courtroom. That man with the gun watching her the whole time, as she pushed slow, unhurried, past tables and chair and people until she got to the defendant. Then she lifted her robes and wrapped them around him. Pulled him in close to her, covering him. Everyone waited for the sound of the shot, the smell of cordite in the air, but it never happened. Nothing happened, except the pistol clattering to the floor, the guards rushing the man, the courtroom spilling outside."

"I'm going to be sick," the mother said.

"Oh, why don't you grow a pair?" said her husband. "Go wait in the car."

Bailey came close but Tate pulled away from her.

"You're damn right I don't understand," he said.

"I wanted to tell you, Daddy, but I didn't know how."

"That's not how I taught you," Tate said. "Especially not with their sort."

"You better watch yourself, old man," shouted the boy from behind his father.

Tate shook his fist at all of them, shouting, "This isn't over. When it ends, I'll end it. And I'll end it simple."

"It wasn't for him, or him, Daddy, or even for that man and his gun. It was for her. I didn't want her to see her father do something like that, something she wouldn't be able to forget."

And Tate saw everything: the girl in the witness box, staring up as her father held the sharp end of a gun between a Judge's eyes, knowing that he would go through with it, that he was ready to rip their world to pieces. Her eyes following Bailey as she crossed the room, as she lifted the robes to wrap the man who had hurt her, as she made it all stop.

"You protected the wrong person, Bailey. You could have covered that little girl's eyes, while her father did what he had to do."

"No, that's what you could have done."

He chopped the air between them with his hands. "No, Bailey. I taught you better than that. How could you?"

"I could because I had to, Dad. I had to because I could."

She leaned into him but he shook his head wildly, his thin arms quaking the glass bottles. He swung his free arm at her, his hand catching her cheek. She fell backward and Tate threw the carton of beers wide, wrapping his fingers around the neck of a single bottle, letting the others drop to the floor, shattering. He pushed Bailey backward until her feet slid, slipped, and she fell into the broken glass. The last thing she saw was her father, the bottle raised over his head, rushing the boy; then her head hit the floor with a loud sound.

II.

Bailey lay flat, blinking. Her body seemed to leach cold from the tile floor as the spinning room gradually rocked to a stop. She listened for voices, but there weren't any. Only a brittle quiet, a silence so thin that it would have been easy to fill, but so complete that it seemed absolute, inviolable. Then the smells of blood and beer saturated the air and she sat up, dripping. Her leg was cut; it was not deep, but the red swirled out of her, curling through the puddled beer.

Nobody was behind the counter. Bailey stood hesitatingly and went from aisle to aisle, crouching to look under shelves, to bend around corners, first calling her father's name, then cursing him softly. The store was empty.

The front doors automatically parted in front of her, letting in the dank suck and draw of evening air. She walked into it and saw that the car was gone. In its empty space was the ginger ale bottle, its cap cracked and hissing. Eggs were smashed like runny suns against the curb.

She heard a sound from around the corner and ran to it, calling "Dad", calling "Tate", but it wasn't her father. It was the boy's mother, kneeling in the grass easement. She fell sideways and Bailey rushed to catch her, holding her upright against the side of the building. The woman turned, her wrinkled face shining, streaked with tears and vomit.

Bailey hushed her in a single, long, seemingly endless breath, her fingers stroking the woman's grey hair back from her face. The woman retched again and they dropped clumsily to their knees in the grass. Bailey cradled the woman's head close to her chest, softly rocking with the arrhythm of the woman's heaving shoulders until the smell overpowered her, and she gagged, and they heaved violently together.

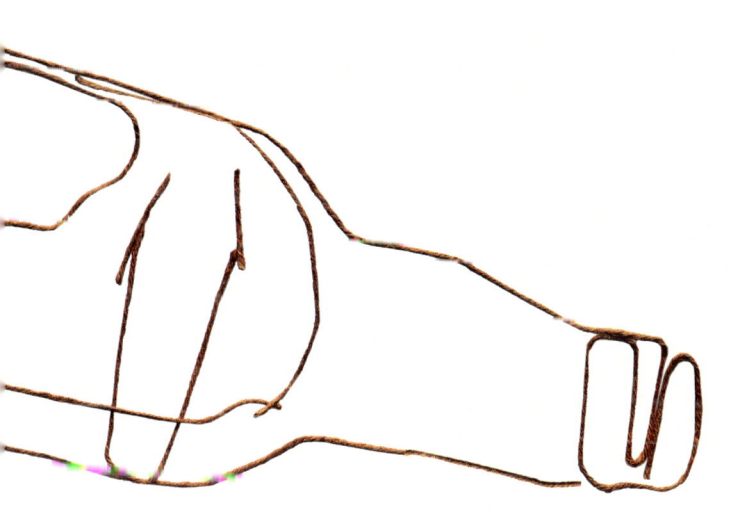

thin king blues

Down the stairs and.
Down the stairs first thing newspaper mornings,
last thing garbage nights.
Back up for dinner or forgotten keys or bed.
Down again to check the mail for checks,
to phone my sister Cookie in Memphis from the payphone,
say How's the flu or Did you get my letter?
Past out and in and upstairs for remembering, downstairs for making.
Down into regret and joy. Even regret a joy to busy long lonely nights,
my mind slow with TV movies and microwave dinners and promises
I practice in the dead quiet after.
Down the stairs and into Bess. Saying, from her doorway,
"Did you ever sit thinking with a thousand things on your mind?
Thinking about someone".
Neighbors should keep apartments locked.
Watch your back door. Close curtains. But she says,
"Don't you hear me baby, knocking on your door? Don't you".
As she squeezes a single tear from her eye. Watching it drop, spinning
mascara black like some forgotten sun, to splash the concrete floor at my.

"It's the only way, baby, I can get these thinking blues off my mind".

Can that be true?
I ask but she won't answer. She only wants something
to grab me and pull me back between the sheets.
Up the stair stair stair stair stair stair stair stair stair stair stair.
The handrail is thin enough for my fingers to wrap all of the way around.
I lose skin off my knuckles on the cinder blocks, every time.
Once I heard that our bodies make all new skin every twenty-four hours.
We are born with each sun and die with the moon,
leaving trails of us on walls, between sheets,
breathed and blown by each other, on every stair.
I don't want to remember this I don't want.
Too many nights down, nearly passing her door, but stopping to knock.
Then long before light, the long walk back up.
She could be only a habit. Like any habit I could try to.
The geographic center of America, once I heard, is somewhere in the
flats of Kansas. A spring bubbles there, but its water is soured from
cross-country campers dumping their shit tanks. I had a friend once
who had a camper, drove it clear across.

"Do you hear me, baby?
Have you got the nerve to say you don't want me no more".

Her words fill the narrow, empty, breezeless stairwell.
If only I can open the door, her words might rush out and be lost in the.
I wish I could paint the stairwell the color of the street and sky.
I wish I could hang a bulb by a worn cord, swinging naked, to set a mood.
I wish I could step outside, past her door, to talk to kind neighbors,
stoop afternoons, wave to families driving past.
And I wish the pipes would rust through, at long last, crack and burst.
That Bess would run, squealing over her laughter, upstairs to my apartment.
We would go together down
and up, down and up again,
carrying dripping heavy cardboard boxes of photos,
bills long past due, an old rug beat thin as paper,

dragging the wet-dry vac
to erase all trace of our wet footprints up the stairs.
Tell someday children that it all changed when her apartment
flooded two inches deep, two.
Change for the bus bulks my pocket.
I saved for months.
It might get me far as Memphis.
I could overnight with Cookie,
borrow more change for the Greyhound's thirsty tank
gulping diesel miles.
For tires that spin bridges that span the Mississippi.
The river at St. Louis nearly a mile wide and muddy,
what starts a trickle somewhere up North, I never.
Then Kansas flat as a bedsheet,
a four-square state, the dry heat heart of the nation.
Watch that bubbling spring, blue and big as any ocean,
blue as thinking, big as
Bess standing in the doorway,
as beautiful as the world is wide as the world is deep
as the world is angry as the world is sharp
as the world is soft as the world is stale
as the world is sweet, calling,

"Take me back, baby, try me one more time.
Don't you hear me, baby".

Bess, I do.
For better for worse for.
Her grinning and dragging the wet-dry vac up
stairs on its retractable cord,
sucking balled cobwebs into the plastic tube.

UNDERLAY

It was still raining—
evening and morning, the
third day. Hal was chewing the knotted
hood-string of his sweatshirt, fraying the braid
between his teeth as the waitress held a hot coffee
pot over Guthrie's head, like a threat.

Guthrie sat without moving, big as the whole booth. His triple-XL jean jacket was still not quite dry after an hour of killing time.

"You should think twice about that, lady," Hal said. "You might be surprised, I've seen him move fast before."

She pretended to be joking and topped off Guthrie's cup. He creased three packets of Domino sugar under his big thumbnail, tore them into his mug, and ordered another apple turnover.

"It's none of my business, mister," she said, her mouth wound in tight disapproval. "But if you start every day like this you're due a heart attack."

He pointed a spoon at her. "If you're calling me fat, just out and say it."

"I didn't say fat."

"Nobody said fat, Guthrie."

"Well, we're all saying it now," he said.

"I didn't mean anything by it," the waitress said. "I could stand to lose a few myself."

"You said it, lady. Not me," Guthrie muttered into the swirling mug.

She stepped backward and put the pot on the counter, out of her own reach. "I'm not sure what that means, mister, but I'm sure I don't like it."

IT WAS STILL RAINING— EVENING AND MORNING, THE THIRD DAY.

Guthrie took a bite and chewed slowly. "It means, not only do you serve shit at this diner but damned if you don't talk it too."

Hal sighed. "Guthrie, what'd you have to say that for?"

"I'd like you to leave," she said, her eyes blackening.

"You can't kick us out."

"What do you mean, us? What'd I do?" asked Hal, glancing at the slate of grey clouds, at the sheeting rain.

"We're paying customers, lady."

"So pay right now. Both of you."

Guthrie was already sliding out of the booth, headed toward the register, twisting his broad mechanic's hand into the pocket of his Levis. He paid for both breakfasts then walked slow back to the table, his huge bald head floating over the booths like a paraded idol, to leave a twenty dollar tip under the ashtray. That's Guthrie's way – always setting things straight, but only after he breaks them.

The last regular job Guthrie had, he was night watchman at the Marriott parking garage. He liked walking the quiet rows of cars to watch over things that he didn't own, that he didn't really worry about. He was in the best shape of his life then, tall and lanky, and during long nights he would race the elevator up and down the stairs for fun. His hair was buzzed short to hide where he was balding, so he looked ex-Military, or like a state trooper, only softer around the eyes. He didn't look like what he was – a man out of Silverdale early for good behavior.

He lost that job because hotel manager's daughter got him fired. One night, a few hours before dawn, she pulled her short blonde SUV into the garage after a bingo down at the brewery. She parked in the handicapped space beside Guthrie's attendant booth, looked him up and down, and tossed him the keys. Then she crawled into the back seat and took off all her clothes.

Guthrie peeped in through the window. She looked out at him, her face pale under his own reflection, and all he could see was trouble. So he dropped the keys on the front seat, locked the doors and walked away as she pressed, furious, against the window.

Before she woke the next morning, one of the kids who worked the breakfast bar walked past, mad at his job, at the hotel, at a world that would allow morning and night to turn just so he could serve limp bacon and toast to travelers. He saw a car in the handicapped parking space without a hang tag on the mirror and, hungry for justice, pulled out his keys to scratch up the car's paint job. But lo and behold, a naked woman was in the back seat, streaks of eyeliner dried down her face. A face he recognized.

She woke up to the chirp of her cell phone and a text message photo of herself, passed out ass-up to the world. She tugged her clothes on and marched inside, telling her daddy that kids will be kids but blaming Guthrie, his name angry spit on her lips. So the manager called Guthrie's house and woke him up just to threaten him, to say don't bother coming back, ever.

Guthrie waited a few days and then hung around the attendant's station after dark. The kid from the breakfast bar, now night watchman, came along proudly shaking Guthrie's old key ring in his pocket, talking on the cell phone. He never saw Guthrie rising out of a shadow to wrap both hands around his collar and pull him into the dark space between two cars.

Guthrie pinned the boy to the pavement with his knees and pulled a folded coat hanger from his pocket, jimmied one of the car doors open. The kid twisted and kicked, struck out, but Guthrie carefully placed the boy's hand, with the phone clenched in it, against the hinge of the open car door and pushed it closed, in no hurry. Crushing until he felt plastic and glass and bone give way. "Let this be a lesson," Guthrie said.

He walked down the garage ramp just as the manager's daughter turned in. He knocked on her window. She said she wouldn't get his job back, but Guthrie told her to pull over, taking the folded coat hanger out of his pocket. She cringed back in the seat, afraid, but Guthrie just slid his hand, slow, easy, along the window seal and showed her how to pop a door lock. She laughed and hit him, playful, across his chest.

He let her choose a couple of luxury sedans in the garage, showed her how to disable an alarm and hotwire an engine. He even let her drive a few, park them in different places than their owners left them. But he wouldn't let her take them out into the street. He didn't want her to get in real trouble, he told Hal later. He just hated to leave her feeling ugly.

Stepping out of the diner, Hal pulled the sleeves of his sweatshirt down over his hands, bunching them in his grip. He was unshaven beneath a dirty baseball cap, the whiskers thickest on his upper lip. He was not tall but was very thin; his mouth often had an expression like he was about to say something, or be sick. He was not graceful as he ran with his chin bent against the cold rain blown sideways on its way to the ground. His hangover made the rain feel like grease and sweat on his skin as he ran with short steps, careful not to fall, and slipped into the back seat of Guthrie's 1953 Mercedes.

Guthrie had bought the car on auction and dropped a modified six-cylinder Chevy engine into it himself, weekend after weekend with Hal passing him wrenches. Hal had never understood its appeal, with the floorboards rusting through under the mats, the seat leather cut and ripped all over. Children in Guthrie's apartment building had torn the Mercedes symbol off the hood, and to Hal, without that chrome peace sign it looked like a clown car.

Guthrie came into the lot, blinking in the rain, pulling an enormous stocking cap down to the collar of a wrinkled camouflage poncho

Hal watched him come close, thinking – good thing the car has room for all three of us. If push comes to shove and the cops show up, or alarms sound, or word somehow gets out, we can park it somewhere hidden and quiet, and have room to stretch out and sleep for a couple days.

In the Saturday quiet of the Southside, the Seventh Day Adventists' prerecorded bells,
tinny and loud, chastised anyone trying to ignore their sabbath.

And every Saturday morning, Hal would bundle his sister Margaret into scarves and blankets, wrapping her securely into the old electric wheelchair and pushing her next door to Miss Bentley's house so he could spend the weekend with Guthrie. Margaret, never talking but never quite quiet, always in the background of family portraits, of his childhood, of his mind.

He would unload her in Miss Bentley's spare bedroom and double-check her cabinets for diabetes and reflux and gas medicines, adult diapers and waterproof ointments and vitamin supplements, making a list of what to buy at the Wal-Mart. Life extended another week by the welfare check, small comforts packed into blue plastic shopping bags.

After their mother died, Hal moved back into the house, thinking that despite its creaks and drafty walls and Margaret it was better than no house at all. But it only took a few weeks before the house seemed to start pulling apart around him – board by board, nail by nail, each pulled one at a time out of its place and sucked along the long hallways into the black hole of Margaret's room. Within a month Hal was bundling her to Miss Bentley's and spending weekends with Guthrie. Guthrie took him in gladly, saying that Hal had earned any bit of fun they could hustle here and there.

Sometimes, at bowling or a bar, people would make comments and implications. One time, Hal backed into a hose at the Fire Hall and sent it sprawling across the garage, and one of the firemen called him faggot. Hal came at him, fists clenched, but Guthrie stepped in between with a serious smile, telling how Hal sets a fork, knife and spoon before Margaret at every meal, even if there is only soup to eat. How he bathes her, and takes her on the bus to the hospital twice a month. And that should tell something about what makes a man. And who wouldn't be lucky to have such a brother.

AFTER THEIR MOTHER DIED, HAL MOVED BACK INTO THE HOUSE.

Hal would sit, listening to them talk about him, waiting to hear something that would tell him what to think of himself. Some hint of a life cracking over the horizon. Hoping to catch one clue, one depth of insight – a story for him to tell himself, and fit the whole world inside of it. Almost any one thing would do, so long as it was big enough to make sense of everything. But it never came. So when they went back to Guthrie's room to sit and watch ESPN for hour after hour, Hal would sit at the far end of the couch, out of reach, but stealing glances at Guthrie, sneaking, delighting.

THE BIG WHITE MERCEDES TURNED OUT OF THE DINER ONTO MAIN STREET, TOWARD DOWNTOWN ⸺ THREE MILES ON THE MAP, MAIN STREET RAN ALONGSIDE THE INTERSTATE, A STRAIGHT LINE FROM ONE T-END TO THE OTHER, FROM WAREHOUSES SURROUNDED BY BROWN BRICK PUBLIC HOUSING TO WAREHOUSES SURROUNDED BY INDUSTRIAL MOONSCAPES THAT BACKED ONTO THE RIVER.

Dead in the middle were four blocks of refurbished lofts and studios and restaurants, art galleries and an artisan grocery, a pocket of promise trying to turn the clock simultaneously forward and backward.

Guthrie slowed to read the posters cluttering shop windows. The Main Street Fall Festival. Local crafts, beer and bratwurst, kiddie carnival rides. A paper banner hung in dripping scraps, the words *World Famous in Chattanooga* running its length. Potholes were swirled with the muddled reflections of store fronts.

Inside, peering out from behind the posters, huddles of three and four people crowded together squinting at the grey sky and holding five-dollar umbrellas with the price tags still on.

"Where in God's earth are all the people?"

"Someplace sunny."

At the Fire Hall, children climbed on wet red trucks as their parents stood in the open bays, scanning the skies for lightning. Dixson had drawn the short straw at work, so he had been stuck in the Fire Hall since sun-up, deep frying donuts for the few tourists who had come by. Now he was standing on the sidewalk, smoking.

"Gentlemen, I have a confession to make," he said, sitting into the front seat and pulling a dry cigarette from a crinkling cellophane packet. "I've got the jitters."

"Me too," said Hal.

"How long has it been, Guthrie? Since you walked into a store and shouted, *Good people of Chattanooga, touch the ceiling.*"

"Not long enough," Guthrie said. "And I don't expect to tonight. No point shouting to an empty building."

Dixson's old man face looked pale and his hands were shaking, just like always. He was a slight man with long sideburns, always fidgeting and shifting in his skin, up late and up early, drinking all night then spending his work days seated on a tall stool in the ready room, scrubbing mops in the deep sink, an unlit cigarette in his fingers, his thin cheeks puffing with effort.

A pee-wee Ferris wheel, no more than twenty feet tall, spun by outside the window.

"There were supposed to be hundreds of people," Dixson said. "They were all supposed to be buying beer and groceries, filling the cash registers."

"Too late to call it off now," said Guthrie.

They stopped at a red light.

"Fair enough," Dixson said. "So what will you do with your share?"

"I don't know how much we'll get, so how can I know how I'll spend it?"

"You're no fun, Guthrie," Dixson said, inhaling hard. "No matter how much it is, I'm headed for Tunica. Turn a bit into a bundle. I found a Blackjack web site written by a math genius, that tells you when to double down, when to stand."

"That's counting cards," Hal said. "Like in that movie with the retard."

"You, of all people, should not use that word."

"Careful," said Guthrie, his eyes widening and slitting.

"Anyway it's not counting cards," Dixson said quickly, changing the subject. "It's playing the overlay. When luck, or God, or whatever smiles on you, instead of the house. Good cards in your hand, real money on the table, odds on your side." He cracked the window to let the smoke out and rain flicked through to the back seat. Hal didn't mind; it felt light and fresh and cool on his face.

"I don't gamble," Guthrie said.

"Won't gamble, or can't? I heard you're banned at every table from St. Louis to Cherokee."

"Not won't. Not can't. Don't."

"He was banned was a long time ago, Dixson," Hal cut in.. "I figure they'd take him back now if he wanted."

They stopped at an empty park playground to piss through the fence. Raindrops beaded on the chain links. Patches of uncut grass bent calisthenic in the wind. They drove back along Main where stores were cutting down the banners and locking up early. In the houses surrounding, yellow living room lights were warm behind doors that had been shut tight against the weather. But Hal was glad to be in the car.

"What'll you spend your money on, Hal?" Dixson asked over the seat, making nice. But Guthrie interrupted: "I guess we all spend on whatever we worry about."

Hal thought, I guess he's right.

Hal knew Guthrie planned to get the stomach staple with his share, and he couldn't help feeling it was his fault. It seemed wrong to him that so much ache, a need for scalpels and stitches, should come from the simple joys of butter and sugar.

During the long weekdays alone in the house with Margaret, living by television, Hal had found cable channel cooking and started preparing elaborate meals for his sister. He would weigh every ingredient, following the chef on the small screen religiously. Soon he was stealing cookbooks from the public library, experimenting with stocks and syrups, teaching himself to julienne and chiffonade in the dark linoleum kitchen. Then he would scrape the plate into a blender, liquefying everything for her to drink it through a washable plastic straw. Morning and night, morning and night, tipping the grey mix to her gaping birdling mouth, her garbage disposal mouth, the all-sucking drain at the back of the house. Day after day, Hal tried to make it into a way to care about caring for her, but no matter what he brought to her, she slurped the same. He tried to resist, to hate hate, to love, but no matter how much he spiced and battered and basted, loaded and unloaded the sink, iced the oven blisters on his fingers and forearms, she took it all and wanted more.

So he started doubling recipes and taking the second plate to Guthrie. Carefully covering plated dishes in cling wrap, carefully wrapping Margaret in blankets and pushing her chair with its dead battery down the street to Guthrie's apartment at the old Days Inn. Before long, Guthrie started opening the door before Hal even knocked, coming outside to eat on the curb between where Hal sat silent and Margaret sat moaning.

In less than one year, Guthrie gained nearly a hundred pounds. Then another seventy. It was as if Hal's extra servings touched off something in him, and he found himself getting up after midnight to drive to drive-thrus. On the weekends when Hal slept on his couch, they went to the grocery together and came out carrying bags

GUTHRIE SOMETIMES BROUGHT GIRLS HOME.

peaked with meats and breads, fresh herbs and new flavors, cases of beer paid for by selling Margaret's food stamps. Guthrie, burly and red-faced, laughing already, sat onto the couch and didn't stand up until the next day, except to stumble into the bathroom. Hal was happy in the kitchen, listening to the TV from the other room as he cooked. Knowing that someone else would be turning Margaret in her bed, wiping her with the washcloth, tipping meals into the whirling tooth of the blender, threading the straw between her colorless lips.

Guthrie sometimes brought girls home, and Hal would curl in his bedroll on the couch, wondering what would happen if he got caught peeking in the bedroom door. One time, Guthrie went for beer and came back with a case under each arm and two girls he had picked up at the bowling alley. Hal was already asleep in his bedroll when they burst into the apartment.

"Want some dessert?" Guthrie called, sitting on the couch. He bent forward, pulling off his shoes and socks. The skin of his ankles showed compression lines and the black hairs were flattened out. He pulled the girl he had chosen for himself into his big lap; the other took Hal by the arm and led him to the bedroom.

"But this isn't my bed," Hal said, and the girl laughed. She was short, the top of her head at Hal's shoulders, and dressed for a night out. Her sequined shirt was too tight across the hips and the tumble of stomach between sweated through the cotton. Her big thighs chafed in the skirt, and her calves ran straight down into her feet, making folds over the tops of her bowling shoes.

"I didn't steal these shoes, I'm in a bowling league," she said. "Plus they're good for my plantar fasciitis."

Her thick, tightly curled hair smelled like plastic fruit. It made Hal feel young and jumpy to sit beside her on the unmade bed.

"When I dressed nice today, I knew there was a reason. That tonight was going to be special." She sat closer, one hand flat on the bed behind him, ready.

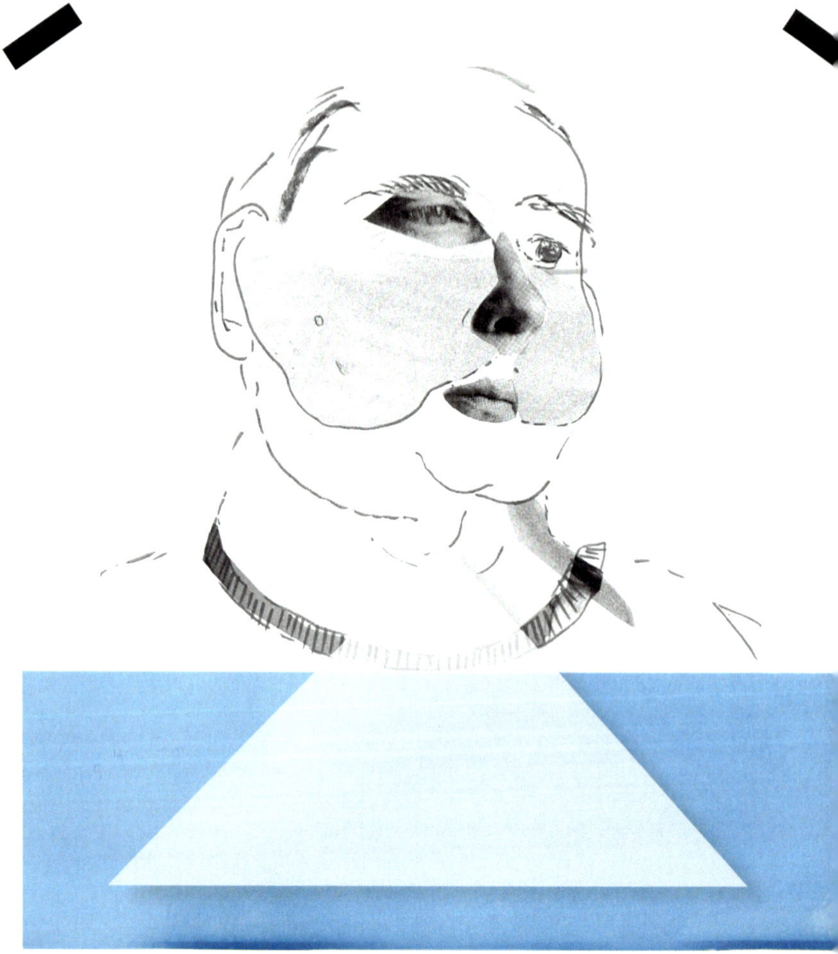

"I don't know," said Hal.

"I'll do you right, Henry. It is Henry, right?"

Hal shrugged.

"Sweet Henry," she said, her hand on his. "Only you have to promise not to look too close. I'm not so pretty naked."

Her arms shook out of the shimmering top, her hair dropping like hushed sunshine through her fingers.

"I think you're very pretty," he said. "It's not that."

"Don't worry, Harry. I don't bleed, on account I'm so heavy. You don't have anything to worry about."

Hal closed his eyes, pretending. Afterward, the girl dressed and immediately left with her friend and a case of beer. Hal lay watching ESPN on one end of the couch as Guthrie made loud sleeping noises from the other. It was less snoring than a deep, painful, hard work of breathing, more groan and gasp than rest. It reminded him of his mother's breathing, always strained, even when he was very small. She would curl up next to his pillow and tell him stories about the Man in the Moon – the jolly face that smiled down proud on all he sees going on below. But for as long as he could remember, when Hal looked at the moon all he could see was Margaret's fat face, her moaning mouth, her eyes wide in horror and unundertanding, stupid to the world's hurt, an idiot child forever confused and afraid.

The next morning Hal took Guthrie to the Bi-Lo, to sit in the car with binoculars. He told how Miss Bentley had been let go from Assistant Manager a few months back, corporate downsizing. She had been angry ever since and would rant for hours over detailed sketches of where they kept the cash box, of stocking timetables and bank runs. Guthrie was unsure until he thought of the Fall Festival, when cash registers would surely be bursting with tourist dollars. Both he and Hal liked the sound of a take big enough to get through winter, maybe even pay for something important.

When Hal woke up, the Mercedes was parked at a gas pump. The hood was up and through the gap Hal could see Guthrie bent over the engine, wearing the camouflage poncho, his hands moving expertly among the dip sticks and fuses.

Dixson slid back into the front seat, a box of longnecks in his lap.

"I bet he checks it every time he fills the tank. Like an old woman."

Guthrie shut the hood and pulled the car around to the back of the station and locked it. They crossed Main Street to Crawford Bros. Tire & Auto. Out front, the low building was crowded with a dozen people under the wide, bright blue awnings. A table had been set up and piled with 8x10 photographs of Murphy Crawford, who was seated behind the table with a signing pen in his hand. He was so tan, he was barely visible against the painted wall behind him. Women were lined up in front of the table, pressed together to stay dry.

Murphy was six foot five, taller than he looked on the TV commercials, with too much mouth and thrilling hair. But he was thin in his shirt after three months in the hospital. His Lexus had been broadsided as he pulled out of his store onto Main Street; it was in the newspaper and on all three local news channels – images of him unconscious, being loaded into the ambulance, his face already bruising; then weeks later, smiling from the hospital bed with a brave thumbs up, then in live video grinning and grimacing on the rehabilitation machines.

Now, just days out of the hospital, he looked out of place in his own clothes. His eyes were too dark to be handsome and his jaw was always working. People came to look, to whisper about what he had looked like before the accident. They said that the photos stacked on the table looked nothing like him.

When he saw Guthrie, Murphy stood from his seat and told the women waiting in line that he needed to take a break. There were compassionate nods all around, so he stood, shook Guthrie's hand and, without letting go, led him into the building. Dixson and Hal followed.

Inside was an office, paneled in painted wood and hung with photographs of fireworks over the river. Against one wall was a desk as wide as the room, stacked with file boxes. Behind it sat a tall man with thick, ringed fingers. Earl Crawford seemed much older than his brother, and wore round metal glasses that made his eyes look rounder than they actually were, like he was always straining to see through the lenses; but when he removed them to wipe them clean, his eyes sunk away in his face. He did not stand or shake hands.

"Isaiah Guthrie," said Murphy, "This is my older brother Earl."

"Did he call you Isaiah?" Earl asked Guthrie.

"Hm," Guthrie said, and shook his head. "Guthrie."

Hal stepped forward, thinking Guthrie would introduce him, but no one moved or spoke. So he looked around for a chair, then leaned back against the wall.

"How do you know my brother, Mr. Guthrie?"

"From around."

"We've known each other a long time," said Murphy. "Everybody knows Guthrie."

"And I guess you two are his boys?"

Dixson said, sure we are.

"Would you mind please not smoking inside? It's bad for business."

"I don't mind," said Dixson, crushing it out.

"You see, women from Cincinnati or Cleveland come to visit our fair city, and they need their oil changed before starting on the long trip home. They don't want to breathe smoke. You understand."

"I don't mind," Dixson said again.

"Mr. Guthrie," Earl said, hesitating, as if he weren't quite sure of how to pronounce the name. "My brother told me your plan, but I'm not sure you're the right man for the job."

"You don't have to be sure of anything. It's not your job," said Guthrie. He stood in the center of the room, framed by the desk, the wall, the men around him, and Hal thought about all the muscle it must take to carry all that weight.

"So why'd you tell your plans to my brother? For the hell of it?"

"More or less," said Guthrie.

"More, or less?"

"It's not like that, Earl," Murphy said from the corner. "When someone buys a pistol out of the trunk of a car on the Southside, word gets to me. To you, I mean, but to me too. Like I said, I know Guthrie, so I thought maybe we can help."

"That's lucky," said Earl.

"Sure it is."

"It's more than lucky, Mr. Guthrie," Earl said. "Because as the very store you're planning to rob is a place we've wanted to get inside for months. The lock box holds an envelope of papers that I want. I don't care how you get it, so long as it lands on this desk."

"I don't remember seeing you in the bushes with binoculars," said Guthrie.

Earl chewed on the eraser end of a pencil, spitting bits of red rubber onto the carpet.

"But you see, Mr. Guthrie, if you break in tomorrow night they will beef up security. New locks, more patrols. So we have two choices. Either you call it off, or you help us out."

"Listen here. No disrespect, but I'm only here as a favor to your brother," Guthrie said.

"Save your favors. We'll give you five grand."

Guthrie stood up straight. "Just for the papers? We keep any cash we find."

"That's none of my business."

"See? Wasn't that easy?" said Murphy.

"Sure it was. Why not."

"Why not," said Guthrie.

Hal couldn't help himself. "What's in the envelope?" he asked.

Guthrie spoke fast for the first time. "Sorry about that, Mr. Crawford. We don't need to know. The way I see things, once I've decided to empty a man's cash drawer I don't object to picking up the mail on the way out. Without opening it."

Dixson pulled a cigarette out of the pack, remembered, stuffed it in his shirt pocket. It broke and tobacco scattered on the floor. He knelt, awkward, brushing the withered leaves into his palm.

"One more question, Mr. Guthrie. You'll forgive me for asking, but are you in shape to pull it off? I don't want you having a heart attack on the doorstep."

Guthrie put both of his hands behind his back. The fingers barely touched. The camouflage poncho flared, its oversized leaves and branches seeming to fill the space, surrounding the desk and walls and men. Damn, Hal thought, he must weigh three hundred pounds. The storm beat on the roof, inches above their heads.

At last Earl said, "Okay. But what if you have to run for it?"

"I don't see that I'll have to."

"Maybe, with a gun in your hand, you have options."

As they drove back down Main Street, Chattanooga Creek was spilling over its bridges. On East 3rd, a car was submerged to its windshield. Another was flipped onto its side, the current turning

MAYBE, WITH A GUN IN YOUR HAND...

the tires and frothing the black underchassis. They drove slowly, watching the water rise like a high tide.

"My brother's house flooded once, in Missouri," Dixson said. "The river filled his house a foot deep. Water swelled up the floorboards and the sheetrock, until the walls crumbled away into nothing."

They stopped for Big Macs and Guthrie paid with his Visa card, calling it a business expense. Dixson asked why the girl at the window why McDonalds doesn't serve beer with dinner, and she said she's looking at three good reasons. They all laughed and she laughed too. She had a dusky laugh that ended in a hoarse cough, a radio sound.

They drove down to the Bi-Lo and sat in the parking lot, eating burgers and digging in the cardboard case until the beers were gone. Much later, they drove across the street and parked at a hotel.

"You got any rooms?"

"How many people?"

"Three."

"Any kids?"

"Just us."

"I don't like this place," Dixson whispered to Hal, too loud, the beer strong on his breath. "Look at that beard. I don't think he's an American." Hal moved away, hoping he wouldn't say it louder. Dixson faded outside, feeling his pockets.

"Two double beds?"

Guthrie glanced at Hal and asked the man, "You have a rollaway?"

"Course we do. That's seventy-five, plus twenty for the rollaway."

"Thanks but no thanks."

"Hold on a minute," the man said. "Maybe you could have a room with two twins and the rollaway, for fifty-five plus twenty."

Guthrie peeled out cash this time, not wanting to use the Visa just across the street from the Bi-Lo.

"What you think of all this rain?" the clerk asked.

"It's a goddamn shame, that's what I think," said Guthrie, then immediately said, "Sorry. I don't mean to be rude. It's just a damn shame."

They walked across the street to the grocery. Out back of the delivery alley, a flooded field was creeping close. Guthrie led them around the building, circling it once, then inside to pick up a case of Michelob and some chips.

The aisles were empty except for a few employees in red vests stocking shelves. Through the big windows, the silhouettes of cars passed now and again. At the check-out the manager walked past, and Guthrie tapped Hal on the arm.

The manager had a potbelly and a high glossy haircut. His nose filled his face, with thin hairs springing from it, and a small mismatched grin. A wide necktie rested on his belly like a sketch of an arrow, pointing vaguely forward. He was a man who spent his life choosing not to be angry at angry customers, angry deliverymen and stock boys, an angry wife and angry children. A life of hiring and scheduling, running inventory and rebudgeting. He walked leaning forward, slightly, following the doubtful arrow on his chest that showed him where to go.

"How are you boys this afternoon?" he asked over the noise of the conveyer belt. "Homes flooded? I hear hotels are filling up."

Hal pretended to look at the covers of the magazines until he couldn't stand it any longer.

"It never rains like this in New York City," he blurted.

"That right? You all from New York City?"

"Sure we are," Hal said.

Dixson shook his head, not looking up.

The manager looked from face to face. "I'm not from here, myself," he said. "Been here five years, although I hardly ever get out of the store. It's a big job, managing a grocery, bigger than people think. You boys get bottled water? The news says don't drink from the tap." Guthrie held up the beer and the manager, always ready to please, said, "Even better. Leave the water for the tourists."

Back in the hotel room with its haphazard paintings on the walls and their shoes piled in a comfortable mess, Dixson and Guthrie stretched out on the twin beds, drinking and watching TV, while Hal unfolded the rollaway. After an hour, Dixson lurched to the bathroom and passed out with his cheek against the toilet seat.

Guthrie said, "I think that maybe you shouldn't have said so much to that manager man."

"He won't remember, by tomorrow."

"He thinks we're out of towners, Hal. We'll come to mind for sure."

"He'll have plenty of other things to think about. He won't remember us at all."

"Maybe. If we're lucky."

"And if he does, we can pay him a visit. Make him forget."

"No, Hal. I don't want any of that sort of thing."

"Then what did you get guns for?"

"I said I got guns, I didn't say I got ammo," Guthrie said. "There's a world of difference, Hal, between blocking a punch and pulling a trigger."

Hal didn't like this. He thought of stories he had heard about Guthrie, young and tall and strong. He thought about the plastic bag under Guthrie's pillow, the pistols inside of it, their perfectly round barrels, the grips for holding on tight. And he realized that he had been thinking about holding a pistol in his hand for weeks, because then he could get what he wanted. It would be as simple as taking it.

"What were you thinking, Hal?" Guthrie laughed without really laughing. "New York City? What the hell."

"I don't know," Hal said, and before he had time to think he added, "Maybe we could go there."

Guthrie stirred to sit up, and Hal thought how much a fat man looks like a baby. He wondered how much money they would have to steal for him to buy two plane tickets, instead of one. Guthrie could use his share for his operation, and Hal could split his share down the middle: two tickets to New York, or even farther. Far away enough for Guthrie to recover, to heal, to grow strong and skinny.

Hal watched him, thinking that this shouldn't be a world of hope, a world of waiting and wondering. Thinking, I don't know what this hope means, and I don't care, but I won't question or poke or prod it. I only know what I want. It's him I want, because he is big as big, big enough for me.

And he thought that now, right now, with Dixson unconscious and unhearing on the bathroom floor, he might tell Guthrie everything he wanted. He built up breath in his lungs.

"How drunk are you, Guthrie?"

"Pretty drunk I guess."

"I mean, if I say something, you think you'll remember?"

"Sure as sober, Hal." Guthrie rolled over so he was facing out the horizontal slash of the window. "Don't say anything you can't unsay."

And all of Hal's want suddenly fell in on him, and he knew that he could only say everything if Guthrie wouldn't remember anything. That he would never tell Guthrie that love is hunger, that hope comes not on a full stomach but on an empty one, one so empty it hurts. And so the only thing left was for the goddamn rain to wash everything away, stores and playgrounds and streets and homes, everything. But that would never happen either, so the only thing left for Hal was to leave, to get out, as far away as quick as possible.

HOW DRUNK ARE YOU, GUTHRIE?

PRETTY DRUNK.

"Why don't we talk about the money, instead? What we can do with it," Guthrie said quietly, looking out the window. "I can get my staple, and Margaret can have her operation, too. If there's only enough for one, if we have to choose, we'll give it to her."

Hal had never talked about an operation for Margaret. There was no surgery, no medicine that could help her.

"But don't you think we'll have to leave town?" Hal said, steadily.

"Why would we leave town?"

"Just to get out and lay low. Even only for a little while."

"You're not talking sense, Hal." Guthrie's voice ricocheted around the room, and he nodded at its echo. "There's something deep inside you, and me, and in Dixson too, something deep down. I don't know if we were born with it, or if it's in the water, or what. But we're not going anywhere. None of us. You might try to claw free, but if you do the very ground around you will shift and shudder, so slow at first you think it's nothing. But then the axis tilts and you slip and slide right back home."

"Wait, what did you say?" Hal said, trying to sit upright, his cheek sticking to the rollaway's thin pillow.

"You just try to pack up and leave, Hal. You'll find I'm right."

"You said you, and me, and Dixson," Hal said, a wet hot core of anger flooding his marrow. "You take it back. He's nothing like you and me, like us."

"Of course he is. It's the three of us, the four with Margaret. That's not such a bad life."

Hal rolled over to push himself to his feet but he couldn't hold himself up. The room twisted and fell away.

"Get some sleep, buddy."

Hal fell onto the foldable bed, staring at the television, hating everything that moved, flat and pixelated, on its screen.

GUTHRIE SHOOK HIM AWAKE JUST BEFORE MIDNIGHT. HAL LAY VERY STILL, WATCHING GUTHRIE UNWRAP TWO PISTOLS FROM NEWSPAPER.

"Only two? Hal doesn't get one?" Dixson asked.

"You don't get one."

"Why the hell not?"

"You told me you won't carry it. Why should I buy three?"

"But what if I had changed my mind?"

"What's changed? They change the law?"

"Heh, I guess not." Dixson told Hal, "If we get caught, all the boys with guns go away for armed robbery. But I'm just a bystander."

"But you'll be right there with us."

"Sure, but what if I'm a hostage?" he asked, and winked.

Guthrie put a shining .380 automatic in the back of his belt and covered it with his jacket. Hal tucked a .32 snub in his pocket and followed them downstairs.

They stopped for beers to take the edge off, then drove past the end of Main, past the edge of downtown, out onto the two lane highways. The yellow lines scrolled up under the tires like a soft hand. Trees blurred past, and looking close Hal thought that he passed through these were woods a hundred times before. The landscape ground around him like mighty unseen gears, the Mercedes spinning at the center, as Guthrie slowed and stopped. He made a three point turn in the middle of the highway and started back the way they had come. Dixson lit one off another. There was no sound but the engine and the fuzzing rain.

They pulled into the Bi-Lo at a quarter past one. Guthrie circled the lot once, like they had made a wrong turn, then drove across the street and parked in the hotel lot. They waited until a police cruiser pulled into the Bi-Lo, right on time. The deputy drove slow past the front doors, then parked under a street light, idling.

"Wasting gas," Dixson said. "That's tax money."

At one-thirty the sheriff disappeared up Main and the three men got out of the Mercedes and crossed the street, skirting the lot and edging around the back of the building. Their shoes splashed the flooded alley. They waited while Dixson took a claw hammer out of his jacket and smashed a window in the delivery doors. Wires embedded in the glass caught and held, but Dixson twisted the hammer and tore them out.

"Looks like a weapon to me," Hal whispered as Dixson reached through the broken glass to unlock the bolt. "You'll get armed robbery sure as I will."

"I didn't think of that." He opened the door and, leaning back against the handle, threw the hammer onto the roof. "Rain washes away fingerprints," he said, winking again, but breathing heavy now.

They waited for their eyes to adjust. Inside, the store was inches deep in water. Security lamps cast the grocery aisles in dim, lifeless light. Guthrie led the way, knowing exactly where to go, white wakes stirred up by his shoes. The store smelled like disinfectant, and newsprint, and the rising stink of the water.

He stopped at a mirrored window at the front of the store and said, over the hum of the freezers, "Give me that claw hammer."

"I left it outside."

Guthrie took the pistol from his belt. "Then give me one of those grocery bags."

"Paper or plastic?" Dixson asked. Nobody laughed.

"Shut up and give me that apron instead."

He wrapped his arm in the red apron and, facing away, shattered the mirrored glass so it powdered and scattered at their feet, coating the apron. Guthrie knocked the last bits clear. Without any signal from Guthrie, Dixson crawled through and came around to unlock the door.

Guthrie went straight through the office, straight for the desk, straight to the drawer that Miss Bentley had described, and lifted from it a cash box the size of a phone book. He took a chisel from his pocket and chipped the lock loose. It popped like a jack in the box and Guthrie pulled out an empty bank bag, a manila folder, and stack after stack of bills in neat rubber bands.

"Lord have mercy," said Dixson. "How much is it?"

"More than we can count standing here."

Guthrie tied the money tight in three plastic bags, then looked close at his chisel edge, checking for nicks.

"I wouldn't worry about that too much, Guthrie," said Hal. "I expect now you can buy another one."

"That for the Crawfords?" Dixson pointed at the manila envelope.

"Looks like it."

"Aren't you a little bit curious?" Dixson asked, taking a cigarette out of his pocket. He cocked the Zippo, but before he could light it, Guthrie said, "Hush. Not a sound."

Hal heard it too – a key in the door, at the far end of the room. The door swung open and a figure came in with a penlight bright in its hand. Dixson and Hal crouched behind two armchairs, but Guthrie stood with nowhere to go, rock still beside the desk. His big green and brown poncho caught the light as it swung, distracted, around the walls. The figure folded down an umbrella.

The rubber grip of the pistol was hot in Hal's hand, coming out of his pocket, pulling his hand along with it.

The penlight shone over the desk, into the empty open drawer. Then Guthrie cleared his throat. The man jumped and fumbled the flashlight, the little circle of light bouncing around the room before stopping on the round mouth of the pistol, then Guthrie's face.

"Get that light out of my eyes," Guthrie said.

It was the manager, his shoulders sloped beneath the open, unbuttoned collar of his raincoat, a thin white t-shirt underneath. Without the tie to point the way, he seemed rudderless. He turned off the flashlight.

"You've got some bad timing."

"It's the flood," the man said, looking up from the gun, trying to place Guthrie's face. He wiped his nose on his sleeve. "There are things I don't want to get washed away."

"I guess not."

"You mind putting that gun down, sir? I don't have one."

"How do I know that?"

"Why would I bring a gun to my own office?"

"Why would you bring a flashlight?"

The manager didn't answer, only reached slowly across the desk and lifted the lid on the cash box. He opened and closed it several times, as though it were a magic trick, a toy with a hidden drawer that would refill again. Then he sat down, his face dark.

"That's a lot of money to keep in a desk drawer," said Guthrie. "Might have been worth making a trip to the bank."

"It's not for the deposit. I've been saving it."

"Why not save it in the bank?"

"It's not exactly mine."

"You stealing from your own store?" Hal asked from behind the chair. The manager started to look around, but Guthrie touched the man's chin with the gun.

"I'm only going to say this once. There's no need for you to look at anyone but me."

"I've seen you already. I remember all three of you, from earlier."

"Now, why would you say something like that?"

"If you let me go, I swear I won't tell it was you."

"That the best you can do?."

"Okay, I can do better. I can not remember. I know how to not remember." The manager leaned into the desk. "I don't remember all the time. Think about it: how do you think I get by? How long do you think a man can work for twenty-seven grand a year? It's a small store, in a small city. I tried to build something here, but regional managers come and go, and never notice us. They forget so easily, that after a couple years you start to wonder – what else will they not notice? A dollar here, a quarter there?"

"You must be a patient man."

"That's true, I am," the manager said. "It's not easy."

"How much you were you saving? How much before you could get out?" Hal called.

"I don't want out," the manager said, not turning. "I want in all the way. I was saving to buy the store. To own it myself. The franchise is looking to close locations anyway, so two years ago I signed with financial backers. They said if I could come up with fifty grand, they'd buy my way out."

"There's more than fifty grand here."

"Hell of a lot more," Dixson said.

"A man has to feed his family, doesn't he? And once I own the place, I won't want to skim anymore."

Sweat shone on Guthrie's face. He wiped it, the shine vanishing under his hand. He chewed the inside of his cheek roughly, thinking, before he spoke.

"You should know something, mister. Earl Crawford wants you out."

"What did you say?" the manager asked, his voice hollow as the vacant store, as the cash box.

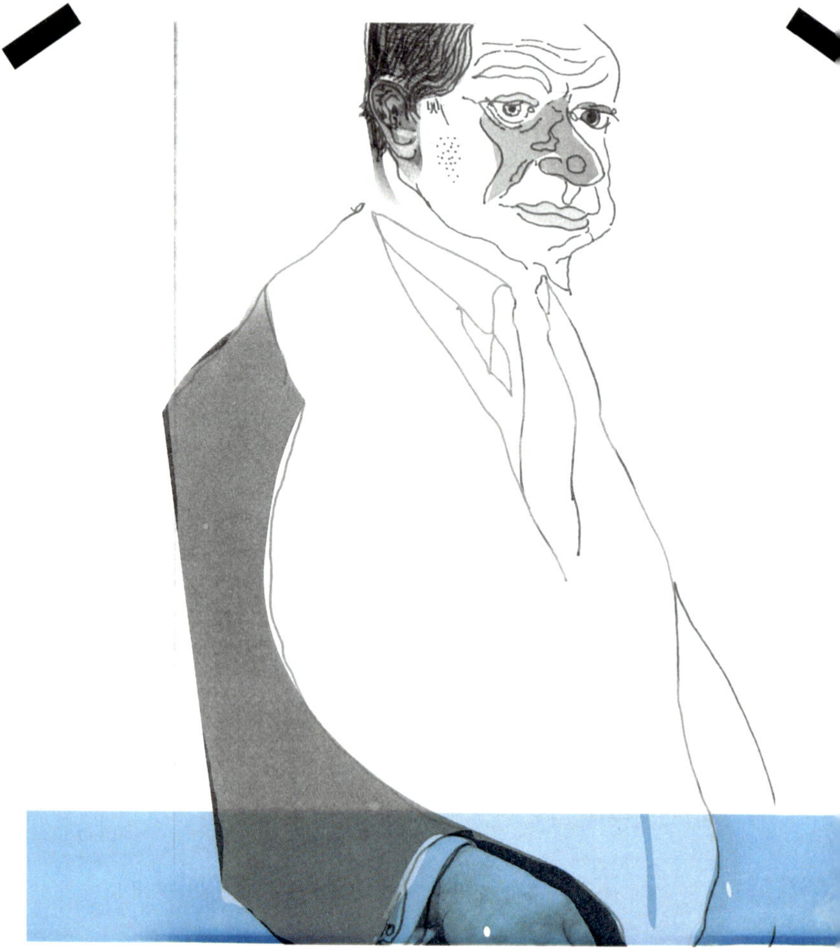

"Why else would he pay me to steal this?"

The penlight snapped up Guthrie's front to the manila envelope, then trembled on Guthrie's chest as the man started to cry, rubbing his cheeks with both hands, rubbing so hard it looked like he might make them bleed. "Oh my God. Am I going to jail?"

"I expect that's the plan."

"But it was their idea in the first place. They said it if I steal, it would make the store look unprofitable, and position us to buy it out."

"I expect they did."

"Oh God, I've got children," the manager said, getting louder. Guthrie set the barrel of the gun, almost gentle, against his cheek, and hushed him. For a few minutes there was no noise but the man's crying. Dixson lit up, inhaled, exhaled. Then Guthrie cleared his throat again.

"What do you want this old place for, anyway?" He sat onto a corner of the desk, the gun barrel still touching the man's face. "By morning it'll have three inches of standing water."

"It's my store," the manager said. "No matter who holds the papers."

"Not if you're locked up."

The man bent forward until his forehead rested against the desk. Hal peeked from around the chair and saw Guthrie sitting over him, looking down, as he reached to wipe the man's tears away with his palm. Then his hand moved fast and hard, tearing the man's raincoat open down the front. Buttons bounced across the desk.

"What are you doing? God, don't shoot me in the chest."

"Sit still, dammit."

Guthrie ripped the t-shirt open, too, down to the belt, then tore open the manila folder with the barrel of the gun. Stapled papers spilled onto the desk.

"Don't do it," Dixson said. "You're pissing away five grand, not to mention pissing off the Crawfords."

"Pick up those papers, and don't say a word," Guthrie said. "Now get out." The manager looked at him. Guthrie stuffed the folder into the man's open shirt, against his white skin. "Keep them dry enough so when you get home you can burn them. Anybody finds those papers, they'll know you were here tonight."

"Oh God," the manager said. "Why?"

"What do you want to ask me that for?"

"You're right," the man said, backing out of the chair, buttoning the raincoat, getting the buttons all wrong, still backing toward the door. "I'm not looking," he said. "I can't see the other two of you." He covered his face with one hand and held the raincoat closed with the other. "I can't see anything."

They followed him to the door and watched him run, without his umbrella, through the rain. His car started and punched out onto Main Street, dropping red streaks from the brake lights onto the gleaming road.

"Sheriff's back in ten minutes," Guthrie said. "And the damn fool forgot his umbrella."

"I'll take it," said Dixson. "No use getting wet."

They hurried back through the store, Guthrie gripping the plastic bags in one hand and the pistol in the other.

At the back door, Dixon raised the umbrella and splashed out, but Hal caught Guthrie by the hand. Holding it, he could feel Guthrie's pulse beneath his fingers.

"What? Be quick."

"Oh Guthrie. What are you going to do?"

"Same as you. Go to the hotel and get some sleep."

"I mean about Crawford. He might come after you."

"We'll tell him the papers weren't here. If that man is smart, he'll say he wants out of the bargain, on account of the flooding."

"If he's smart."

"Yeah, maybe I should have told him that," Guthrie said and stepped outside. His mouth was tight at the corners, and when he spoke it seemed to Hal that everything went quiet, that he breathed the wind out of the sky. "Did you see all that money? There might be enough."

"Yes," Hal whispered.

"Or maybe there's other ways to help Margaret."

"No."

"What no?"

Because Hal knew the way to help her was the straw and the blender and baths and turning her in bed, morning and evening, morning and evening, always the next day.

"We should go, Guthrie."

"That's what I'm saying."

"I mean away. From everything. All of it."

Hal waved his hand like he was parting the rain, holding back the waters.

"Leave? Hell, Hal, where would you go?"

Guthrie turned and splashed toward the hotel. As Hal followed, his steps stuttering in backbeat to Guthrie's, he imagined creeks rising higher and higher, fed from deep unseen springs, from far-off rivers and oceans, rising as high as the sky, wiping everything away under the idiot face of the moon, leaving nothing.

THE NEXT MORNING HAL WAS AT THE AIRPORT, SITTING AT THE BAR UNDER THE LITTLE ROTUNDA. HE HAD WAITED AROUND BAGGAGE CLAIM AND THE GIFT SHOP FOR MORE THAN AN HOUR, BUT HADN'T SEEN ANYONE WHO LOOKED RIGHT.

But now, he sat with his back to a man who was traveling alone. The man was about his age, unshaven, with a tired stare. Every few minutes he turned in his seat to catch Hal's eye.

Hal let him look, rubbing his chin as if he were lost in thought, slipping his fingertip into his mouth. He hated every moment of it, thinking that he might as well slip that finger on down his throat and puke all over the bar top. Hating it as much as he had hated wrapping the bundled cash in a plastic bag, then wrapping the bag in duct tape so Margaret couldn't tear it open, then taping it to her arm. As much as he had hated pushing her into the bright lights of the emergency room lobby, locking the wheels and walking away fast to hide in the bushes outside and watch until the orderlies found her. Telling himself that whoever finds her finds the money will keep it for her will care for her.

The man stood from the bar and came over to him.

"Nice day," he said.

"It could be," Hal replied.

He forced himself to look at the man's mouth. And when the man stepped away toward the bathroom, glancing back, Hal followed. He went into the bathroom and stood at a urinal as the man went into a stall, waiting until they were alone.

Hal knocked at the stall door, and when the man opened it he was standing with his pants around his ankles. Hal punched him hard in the face, once, twice, aiming for his eyes. The man fell backward against the cool tile and Hal grabbed at his shirt, pulling him upright to hit him again, aiming for the blood.

"If you follow me, I will find your wife, your friends, your boss, your preacher, and I will tell them what you wanted," Hal whispered, his mouth inches from the man's ear. He fumbled through the man's pockets and found a wallet, pulled out his driver's license. "See this? I have it. I know your name, and I will use it." The man's eyes were shut tight, already swelling, and he shook his head so hard that blood spattered Hal's shirt. "If you follow me, if you take even one step in my direction, I will come after you for as long as I live, trailing ruin behind me."

He rummaged in the man's bag for the ticket printed with the airline name, the flight and seat number, not bothering to search for the destination. He could hardly feel the paper between his fingers. He glanced again at the man's driver's license. The picture was close enough.

"I will not say I'm sorry to you," he told the man, bending low over him, shaking in his face. "I don't even know you. I will never say it."

He washed his hands as best he could in the sink and pulled the man's coat on, holding it closed over the blood. In the concourse he heard the intercom, found the flight number, heard the final boarding call. He waited in line surrounded by people who were chatting, gathering children, texting loved ones that they would be home soon. He handed the ticket and the license to the attendant.

"I've had a haircut since that picture was taken."

Her smile was empty and quick, a move-along-please smile. He walked fast down the jetway. Words were printed on the carpet in scuffed paint. At the end of the tunnel were stairs down to the tarmac. At the foot of the stairs was the blue and white plane. And from there, wherever.

Behind him, a woman with heavy suitcases said, "Will you hurry up please?"

But he stood without moving, would not even take the first stair, for no reason that he could think of.

CANTATA 82

THE FIRST TIME SHE FELL, Anna thought: maybe everything that's beautiful starts ugly. Three stories of brick rushing past her, once nothing but dirty sand. The snow rising spotless to meet her, once gasoline-swirled puddles in parking lots. Even her own body, twisting through the air toward the ground, once nothing but a raisin-faced newborn, with all her future joy and fear and sex and death out on the birthing table for anyone to see. Not yet repressed deep into the DNA.

The paint can hit the ground before she did, popping open in a splash. She lay on her side in the paint and snow for a long time before anyone noticed. When the ambulance loaded her inside, the EMTs bent over her, then made notes on the scene: cables dangling from the maintenance panel on the roof, spilled paint can and wet brush, tool belt of pliers and wire cutters still strapped around her waist.

As the ambulance shuddered and the streets slid past, Anna muttered through the morphine: damned bricklayers, always throwing up buildings, stealing pieces of sky. What was uncluttered blue now cut into clean geometries of cornices and ridge poles. When it was a vacant lot, empty except for grass and trash, people walking through the neighborhood would stop to stare at the morning moon or watch clouds make shapes in broken bits of glass. Night in day, sky in ground, all crammed into half an acre of nothing much. Now there's nothing there but a building. The EMTs were used to ignoring ramblings from the gurney, and went about their paperwork.

A week later, after the needles and skin grafts and sticky nausea, Anna came back to the church. Two days of blowy, early February rain had melted the snow, leaving only mounded bumpers of mottled brown and white at the edge of the street. Down the front face of the building, a long streak of mismatched paint showed on the brick, covering over the places where she had bounced off the wall on her way to the ground. The doctor said that very well could be what had saved her – the weight of her body pressing into the rough brick as she fell, the friction of her fighting gravity.

"Simeon Schaeffer?"

"PFC Simeon Schaeffer."

"I'm aware of your rank," said the petty officer seated behind the desk. "Sit down and I'll let him know you're here."

Simeon sat on the bench, at the end closest to the door. His back touched the wall behind him at the shoulder blades. Like the wall has just been painted, he thought, and my uniform is stuck to it only at these two points.

Ten minutes later the officer called him. "You, Schaeffer. Go into the first room and strip down to your shorts. He'll be in to see you soon."

"Do you have any idea of how long it will take?" Simeon asked. "My sergeant told me to report in an hour."

"Don't worry, you won't wait long."

"Should I come back tomorrow?"

"Go on back, private," the man said, emphasizing the rank. "He's with other patients, he'll be there in a minute."

The heels of Simeon's shoes struck the floor slowly,

trying to mark intervals of one second exactly without glancing at his watch. He closed the door to the small room and stripped, feeling his shoulders come square out of the undershirt. He thought about how much he would miss wearing the uniforms, seeing the mixture of admiration and apprehension in friends and strangers. Before leaving for Basic, he had worn MultiCam to his high school reunion, among the bowties and suspenders of his old classmates. Stopping to chat with spotty, spangle-eyed middle schoolers in the school halls.

"High school reunions," said Hunter, who had once been his best friend and was now a corporate recruiter in Charlotte, showing off his pop psychology. "Who cares, much less remembers. Only the fat ones, the ugly ones, the timid and unfastened ones."

But Simeon hadn't been able to agree. He was glad to see old friends, to meet the wives and children on their arms. All politely avoiding talk of Betsy, asking about life in the Army, avoiding all talk of wars.

"At ease," the medical officer said when he arrived, not glancing up from the chart in his hand. "Schaeffer, PFC?"

"Yes, sir."

He flipped the chart. "How long have you been in?"

"Six months." Simeon stood awkwardly at ease in his underwear, his legs jutting out of the white briefs.

"Hometown?"

"Atlanta."

The officer smiled at the chart, a brief flash. "And you're old, private. Not a typical recruit just out of high school. Where'd you come from?"

"Seminary, sir."

The officer tapped his teeth with the tip of the pen. Ink rubbed off on his front teeth.

"Lie back."

He palpated Simeon's abdomen with deft circling fingers.

"I knew a sculptor, once, who went to seminary just so he could say he dropped out. The failed priest factor is good with the ladies. Very Van Gogh."

"I graduated," Simeon said as the man dug a thumb into his kidneys, his liver.

"So why not enlist as a chaplain?"

Simeon held his breath with each prodding shove, answering in short spurts. "I don't know, sir. Lots of reasons."

The officer's hand stopped, but didn't lift away from Simeon's stomach.

"This isn't small talk, Schaeffer. I asked you a question."

"Yes, sir. A chaplain has a ministry of presence, going where the soldiers go. No offence meant to the chaplains corps, but that didn't seem like enough to me."

"Do what the grunts do."

"Yes, sir. To be with them, I have to be one of them."

The officer unwound the stethoscope from his neck. Simeon breathed deeply when the man told him to, thinking: how can he listen to my heartbeat and my lungs and my answers all at once?

"I get that, I respect that. But why the Army at all? They have girls at that seminary of yours? You have girl trouble?"

Simeon thought of the letter folded at the bottom of his dresser drawer, back in barracks. Of Betsy's handwriting, large and looping and desperate; words he read every night, following the pen line with his eyes to try to burn them into the paper, to keep them from disappearing. He thought of standing on the balcony watching her walk up the icy hill above the ski lodge with some Australian shitkicker whose name he didn't know. They were wearing nothing but ski boots, carrying big baking sheets stolen from the hotel kitchen. His fiancée, walking naked on a hill with a man he'd never know. And then they came sledding down fast, Betsy out front, snow pluming high behind the sides of the trey, her eyes shut. She twisted to a stop under the balcony and stood up, bleeding from her knuckles. The Australian, close behind on his trey, slid into the wall of the lodge, jumped up and hurried inside. But Betsy stood like a tall stack of plates, her skin blotched with the cold, not bothering to cover herself. She stared up at Simeon on the balcony. From another window, a camera flash blinked the snow around her into painful white. That was the last time he ever saw her. How can that happen, in this day and age, Simeon wondered as he lay under the doctor's hands, that you can never see someone again.

"I just needed a change."

"Well, you came to the right place."

"At least here I know what to do, sir."

"Explain. Cough."

Simeon coughed so deep in his throat that his lungs rattled.

"Here, I am told exactly what to do. And when, and where, and for how long."

The officer frowned. "We don't want robots, private. We want you to think."

"Just not for ourselves."

The officer came around the table to face Simeon, chuckling. "You might have a point."

Simeon didn't want to talk any more.

"It really was that simple, sir. I needed a change."

"Well, let's see if you're about to get another one."

The doctor spent a long time peering into Simeon's ears. The stethoscope hung from his chest, its bright blue rubber tubes converging at the metal listening disc that hung in front of Simeon's mouth, as if the man were recording every word. Simeon could still feel the cold prints where the disc had rested against his skin.

"Passed out three times in six months?"

Simeon nodded.

"You tested clean for drugs and your CT is clear. Are you hydrating?"

"Yes sir, confirmed by my sergeant. He says if a soldier died from heat stroke, it would be a black mark on his record."

"Not just his." The officer scratched his temple with

the pen, leaving staccato dashes of black just outside his hairline. "So do you like the idea of fighting, Schaeffer?"

"I'm sorry, sir. I'm not sure I understand."

"Does it inspire you, thrill you? Are you the hammer of God, bringing judgment on the infidel?"

"No, sir. I don't want to do that. Not unless I have to."

"You mean, unless you're ordered."

"Right. Unless I'm ordered."

"But it must at least inspire you. Remember, I said inspire, too." He waved the stethoscope in the air like a baton, like a bayonet. "You know, 1812 Overture, your own personal handheld cannon blasting in cadence."

In basic training, Simeon's troop had rushed the South Carolina sand pits in waves, jumping in to battle life-size dummies on ropes. They slashed with the same field knives carried by thousands of recruits before them, gashing throats and bellies, the mannequin enemy bleeding sawdust onto their faces their hands, into their mouths. When Simeon collapsed for the third time it was in one of these pits. He sagged forward onto a dummy, sliding down its loose form to sink his hands deep into the hot sand, digging for the cold soil that he knew must be somewhere underneath. His mind wandered among the boots that stomped and kicked around him, thinking that if only he could bury his hands deep enough, he might get stuck. So they would leave him lying there until he shriveled in the August sun, invisible and immaterial, just another obstacle for the next wave of recruits to clamber over. He woke in the base hospital with a dozen interns and nurses crowding the bed. He lay very still, thinking that he had never felt more a part of the Army than at that moment, with them grouped around him, lifting his eyelids and poking specula into his ears, plumping his veins, reviving him. So he straightened his back, obedient to every request, returning their stares and answering their questions, straining to hold his body at attention against the thin mattress.

"That's not why I joined," Simeon said.

The doctor lowered the metal disc in denouement.

"Do you know what the 1812 Overture is?"

Simeon's head filled with the score's bellowing brass crescendo. He wanted to end the conversation, the examination, thinking that he couldn't be late, couldn't keep the sergeant waiting. He shrugged, unwilling to lie. The doctor laughed aloud, reassured in his love for Tchaikovsky that he was more than just a doctor, and dropped the stethoscope. The earplugs slipped out of his ears and snapped together around his neck.

"All right, private. I get a lot of bullshitters in here, kids eager to get out of uniform. It's my job to report on whether they're a danger to society. Are you a danger to society?"

"No, sir. And I'm not eager to get out of my uniform."

"Okay, then we're finished."

Simeon reached for his clothes, getting up.

"How much longer do I have?" he asked.

The doctor grinned.

"Don't sound so worried, Schaeffer, Jesus isn't calling. Get your heart checked once a year, take whatever meds they give you. You'll have a long, full life. You just can't have it in combat."

"No, sir. I mean until I'm discharged."

"Oh, that. Four, five days at the most. Want me to recommend a desk job?"

"Thank you, sir, but I'll reenlist as chaplain."

"I don't think so. A chaplain's job is to carry soldiers in the field, not for them to carry you."

As the medical officer stepped out into the hallway, Simeon leaned after him.

"Sir, excuse me, sir?"

The man was surprised at being called back, the next soldier's chart already open on the clipboard.

"What will I do?"

The officer paused, thinking.

"Can't you go home?"

Simeon thought of flying into Atlanta, walking the terminal corridors of Hartsfield without the uniform. Feeling as naked in civvies as if he were walking through the hallways in briefs, everyone staring or politely looking the other way. He shook his head.

"Give it some time, son. Pick a city that's close but not too close, familiar but not too familiar. Smaller than home, more manageable." He laughed again, looking at Simeon's expression. "And don't worry, I'm sure you can find someone to tell you exactly what to do."

Simeon began to dress even before the door closed. He unshaped the undershirt from the hanger, feeling the cotton catch against his short, coarse hair as he pulled it over his head. Next, the collared, starched white shirt, its six buttons sliding into place. His fingers worked fast, hoping that an hour hadn't passed, so he could report to the sergeant on time.

But as he walked from the base hospital to his barracks, he found himself refusing rides from passing trucks, slowing his walk, hoping that he was late. That the sergeant would shout at him, roaring inches from his face.

And if he tells me to scrub the floors, I will do it. And if he tells me to groan through a thousand pushups, I will do it. And if he tells me to stand stock-still in the center of the room, I will do it.

THE NEW CHURCH BUILDING was three stories of red brick on the Southside of downtown, tucked between businesses and backing onto homes. Within walking distance of everything, it stood opposite a bank square crowded with pigeons, on the site of a once-grand hotel that had been passed over by the renovation revival that swept Chattanooga for much of the 1990s. Constructed on a perfectly square footprint, the hotel's interior balconies towered over a central atrium, ten floors up to skylights; a decade earlier, the atrium had caught the eye of a Hollywood location scout, who strung cables over the ornate indoor fountain, and for one week the lobby was hung with a minor action star and his love interest, swinging to safety. The city's newspaper printed a story about which restaurants the stars visited and their photo-op walks in the park on the anniversary of the film's release, for years, and celluloid prints were blown up and hung in poster frames in the hotel lobby. But none of this could save the hotel from swelling plywood in the windows and, eventually, a controlled blast at its thick, load-bearing columns.

The lot sat empty at the corner of Main and Washington, rubbled, collecting trash until Braxton Jackson muscled a picnic table onto the lot and sat down with four neighborhood families to hold an outdoor worship service. Braxton, forty-four and with a thick brown goatee, had once been an athlete, high school or college soccer, but his body had since slipped into a stubborn atrophy. When he leaned forward against the picnic table to pray or lay out the communion meal of Bunny Bread and grape juice, his back arched forward so that his stomach lipped over his belt. His voice was Southern syrup, his grip reassuring, his face fleshy under an immaculate baseball cap. He held hands with the others and loudly thanked God that the lot was strategically located in an area of downtown that was filled with Sunday morning walkers, who stopped to watch as they held hands, their heads bowed.

Braxton stood on the picnic table for the sermon, preached looking backward at twenty-five years of genocide and global warming, Y2K and the Towers, rumors of AIDS replaced with rumors of West Nile and mad cow and SARS and bird flu, pesticided vegetables on plates and bubbles in bank accounts. Our lives have become transparent, he said. Our parents thought they lived in a simpler time, afraid only of war and fear itself, but it's we who have become simple. The only thing we have to fear is everything. The Far East, the Middle East, Wall Street, nuclear fallout, chemical spills, bacteria, antibacterials, public schools, private schools, the mind games of other churches. We're baby beasts cowering in the corner, every day facing annihilation. Put locks on your doors, on your children, on your water and your air.

Membership skyrocketed. When they hit one hundred people, Braxton bought a speakers' podium off of Craigslist. When they hit two hundred, he bought four silver plates for the offertory, trading up from a lidless coffee tin, and splurged on artisan bread and ten dollar wine for communion. Around the time that Anna started attending services, the church had moved into a bakery that was closed Sundays, for $50 a week plus clean-up. Walking to the bakery before the morning service, she would stop at the empty lot to think that she had liked meeting there, gathered in a circle around the edge of the lot with their backs against the fence. Because while they prayed, she would stare at the morning moon and broken clouds, at the thin weeds pushing through hairline cracks in the street, patiently crumbling the asphalt from underneath.

INTERNS FIRST ARRIVED from seminaries in Mississippi, St. Louis and Philadelphia, come to build strong resumés as junior pastors *cum* entrepreneurs *cum* community organizers. Older parishoners started neighborhood service groups, feeding homeless men or volunteering at a public health clinic. At their head was deaconess Estelle Moffatt, whose house was the first and largest in the neighborhood, whose father had sold off parcels of his land to friends who became neighbors. At seventy-three years old, she was still a squat and capable woman, built for action, her arms loose and thin in their sleeves. Her eyes were small and wary as snails. Whenever she smiled she was making plans, right up until the moment that she caught the fever that escalated and spread until she died.

At her funeral, Mrs. Moffat's son stood up to announce that his mother had willed the lot at Main and Washington to the church, along with five smaller lots to be sold immediately, with proceeds going toward construction. The sales brought an astonishing amount, enough for Braxton to form a capital campaign committee, secure loans and buy a brass shovel. Anna stopped by the construction site every morning to watch a floor shaped out of slab, rebar skeleton upward, bricks rise against the sky. Ten floor-to-ceiling stained glass windows were set into the walls, technicolor prophets veined with thick lines of lead. The newly laid sod smelled like ashes.

A prefab steeple was assembled on the lawn, then raised on a crane. Anna stood at the fluttering caution tape, talking about how they didn't need a building, didn't need a steeple, but Braxton disagreed. He said that a spire is a symbol that raises the church above the everyday. There is no such thing as above the everyday, Anna protested, but Braxton thrilled about driving through downtown, seeing steeples scattered like mile markers of God's progress throughout the city. Then one of the contractors, eavesdropping on their conversation, pointed out that a cell phone tower can be embedded in a church steeple's hollow interior –

a revenue stream to offset monthly budgets.

Damned clever bricklayers, Anna thought.

So she waited, biding her time as the blush of summer turned chill, until sun followed by ice rumpled the paint at the base of the steeple. One snowy February morning, brush and can in hand, she climbed a steel ladder that was bolted to the wall at the back of the sanctuary, discreetly hidden behind the pulpit. Up on the roof, Anna pretended to paint the blistered paint as she thrust her arm deep inside a maintenance panel, tugging at the cables, at the creeping cancer of cell phone signals spreading across the neighborhood. Pulling so hard that when they tore free, she lost her balance on a patch of ice, and fell thirty feet down to the snow in a splash of white.

THE TAXI WINDOW WAS SCARRED with clumsy initials scratched by pens or penknives into the glass, restless moments of restless passengers. Simeon slouched bored against the seat, watching the highway burn past from the airport to downtown, until he caught the first glimpse of downtown. The handful of squat skyscrapers and parking garages scattered along the S-curve of the river. The last evening sun caught at the top corners of the tallest buildings, thirty stories up, bright as fragmenting glass.

Braxton stood on the church's front lawn, kicking at the edge of a slabs of sod as the taxi slowed to a stop. He led Simeon through the front door with its small, tidy vinyl letters: no smoking or weapons on the premises. Braxton's office was still stacked with cardboard boxes.

"I should thank you, Simeon, for accepting the internship

without a visit. Church budgets, you know."

He spoke slowly, a patient man, patient with himself, with his own voice from the pulpit.

"Our last pastoral intern just left, and to be honest I'm not sorry to see him go. He was never much for rolling up his sleeves and getting to work. But your commanding officer said you're quite willing to work hard."

"That's true," Simeon said.

"Good enough for Uncle Sam, good enough for me." He passed Simeon a key on a plastic chain. "There's a furnished apartment in the basement, simple but adequate if you call a bed, shelves and a hot plate furnished. It's yours if you want it."

Simeon's first days at the church were spent unpacking boxes of books into shelves that smelled strongly of new paint. On his fourth day, he was still cataloguing titles on homiletics when a man knocked on the door jamb, wearing a green jumpsuit.

"The preacher sent me down here, said you're the man to see." He held a folded brochure that showed smiling workers on lawnmowers, giving a thumbs up to the camera. "We give superior service, without the bureaucratic bullshit," he said, gauging how much to bid for the job based on how much Simeon flinched at curse words.

"Do other lawn services have a lot of bureaucracy?"

"I wouldn't know," he snapped, "I don't work for them."

Simeon held up both hands, palms forward. "You're kind to think of us," he said, "but I think we'd rather pay kids in the neighborhood to do the yard work. I'm sure someone in the congregation has an old push mower."

The man raised the window blinds. Other jumpsuits were wheeling mowers in a crisscross pattern over the lawn.

"You know that's sod, right?" Simeon said, trying to speak lightly. "I don't think it's even rooted yet."

"First time is free," the man said. "Don't answer now, think on it a couple days."

As soon as he left, Simeon called the number on the brochure. He explained to the voicemail that the last thing a church needs is a service that the homes and businesses surrounding don't have. A church should be an ordinary part of the neighborhood, like any laundromat or taqueria or furniture store. The next morning he received a letter of apology, hand-delivered by a project foreman, promising better attention to detail. Behind him in the alley, the jumpsuits rounded newly-planted boxwoods with roaring, gas-powered trimmers. Simeon left another voicemail and received a 10% off coupon. Sent a letter, got a fruit basket. They had shown up every week since, to trim hedges that were already trimmed, pressure wash the already-immaculate façade of the building, edge the sidewalks.

But Simeon would not let them touch the hedge that ran from the back door to the street. It was an old pine hedge, thick twisted with needles and five feet tall – the only bush or tree on the lot that had not been imported in burlap bags. Simeon trimmed it himself with hand clippers, sweeping the sticks into black plastic bags and swinging them over his shoulder to carry them, like a sweating Santa, through the alley to the curb.

SUNDAY AFTER SUNDAY, Simeon took three steps up onto the platform at the front of the sanctuary, to sit behind Braxton as he preached. Looked out at the pews at people fighting yawns for half an hour, then took three steps down to stand among them. To pass them on sidewalks, in schools and coffee shops, in waiting rooms and conference rooms and living rooms, anywhere they would let him.

Some Sundays, Simeon spent the entire day in the sanctuary, in an endless round of handshakes and lunch invitations, polite questions framed as answers, answers framed as questions. The sun hit the stained glass windows, bursting the figures into reds and blues that played, slowly, across the walls. After the evening service and choir practice, the sanctuary would clear and Simeon would lock the door. Then he would stand praying, his hands over the white cloth covered communion table, thinking of the moment, once a week, when he held the plate and cup up in the air in front of the congregation. This was his favorite part of the service: lifting bread and wine between earth and heaven, God in the cup, and his people coming forward with faces excited and unburdened and uncertain, taking something too big to hold in their hands, too big to eat in their mouths. Standing alone in the dark sanctuary, he would pray until his head drooped. And then, instead of returning to the small bare basement apartment, he would unroll a sleeping bag onto the hard pew, to sleep under the fading notes of voices still fluttering in the rafters.

THE FIRST TIME HE SAW ANNA, she was silhouetted against the sidewalk, avoiding her reflection in store windows. One of the deacons' wives saw him watching her and whispered not to stare, telling him how Anna had been an English teacher at the Christian college prep school until a year before – until a surprise pregnancy, until her husband decided he was not ready to become a father and vanished down the highway to Atlanta. How she offered the baby, still in her stomach, to a sterile university professor and his tragic wife. Anna paid all of the OB and epidural and hospital costs herself, saying that the couple should save their money, or invest it in a college fund.

Simeon shushed the woman, saying that this should be Anna's to tell. But the woman kept talking – telling of a child born dead, the couple left childless in the waiting room and Anna spent and empty, tearing the IV out of her arm and slamming her hands in a drawer until they were broken and bleeding, until the nurses pushed her against the wall and filled her with Versed.

Every day after work while the church was being built, Anna would stand at the edge of the construction site long into the night. The neighbors told Braxton and he took her coffee, told her to go home, but she would only ask him to stop construction, saying that bricks and pews wouldn't bring God any closer. She tried to block the crane as it lifted the steeple swinging in the air, and Braxton threatened to ban her from the premises, including Sunday services. So she retracted and said that she wouldn't interfere again, but only if he would let her clean the church building every night. That she couldn't sleep anyway, and might as well serve her brothers and sisters in this way. Braxton relented, agreed, and installed security cameras in the corridors.

WHEN SIMEON GREETED ANNA at the church's front door after each service, she wouldn't look up. She stood balanced, her hands clasped at the waist, while Sunday School boys circled back for another look. The sheer drop of her dress, the curves of her clothes, the purple jelly stripes of scars like veins on the backs of her hands. Simeon watched her as she walked past him, thinking that he knew her doubts, her questions, her questioning of her questions.

    He always avoided her in the hallways, carrying a book in case he ran into her late nights when they were alone in the church, as she pushed a mop bucket or wheeled trash can over the quiet carpet. But on Sundays he could sit behind the pulpit and stare at her without being chided, watching her wedged into the corner of a pew near the back of the sanctuary, her feet pulled up underneath her. She never stood for prayers or hymns with the rest of the congregation; instead, she sat with her cheek against her arm, her eyes shifting under the lids.

concentrating, her mouth shaping the words utterly, ecstatically.

And then it seemed to Simeon that he saw her everywhere. Anna at every bus stop, in every street, in every store or restaurant. Maybe she had always been there, he thought, at the margins of his seeing until the world shifted and shook her into view. Until his eyes focused at the right place, at the right moment, and he saw her. Her hair long, her skin shades of brown on brown like a Sunday suit. Her mouth, always without makeup, the color of ripening fruit. Even when he prayed, she was there, stitched into the backs of his eyelids.

And he wondered if she might be why he had come to Chattanooga – for one girl on the sidewalk. For Anna, always walking fast from one thing to another, her steps too soft to hear from a distance. Tired Anna, lovely Anna, her hair always loose and unbrushed; her clothes practical and unadorned, loose jeans and tennis shoes. And, now that the weather had turned cold, a knee-length grey coat unbuttoned so it swung in arcs with each step, like great and colorless wings. She never walked in a straight line and, although he wasn't sure, from a distance Simeon thought she might be walking with her eyes closed.

"So will you listen now?" Braxton asked her. "It's one thing for you to dust and vacuum, but quite another for you to strap on a carpenter's belt and work on the steeple. If we need something painted, we've got a lawn service."

"Actually, you don't," she said, thinking of the unsigned contract she had seen on Simeon's desk.

"Of course we do, I've seen them. They're very professional."

"I'm sure they'd be glad to hear it."

"Don't take a tone, Anna," Braxton said. "I'm not saying it's inappropriate for a woman to play carpenter, or climb on the roof like a monkey. I shouldn't have to." He tried to speak kindly, folding one tanned hand over the other, a practiced gesture. "We're trying to make a good impression on the neighborhood. What message does it send if they look out the windows and see our people falling off the roof, bleeding in the front lawn, being carried off in an ambulance?"

Anna watched the pastor as he talked; standing against a backdrop of flower arrangements in the foyer, he looked like a portrait, flat and foregrounded, meticulously lined. In her periphery, Simeon was watching, warming the front pew.

"We don't want you hurt, Anna; there are so many liabilities. Although if you'd only let us pay you, you'd be an employee. And then if something happened, we could help you better."

"I told you when I started, Braxton. I can't sleep, so I might as well be useful."

"Maybe you should see a doctor. You're a young woman. You should be out having fun, not scrubbing a church."

"It's not a church, Braxton, it's a building. The people are the church."

"Yes, yes. You've said all of that before," he muttered, clipping the words. "You know what I mean."

Anna wanted the conversation to be over, so she ducked her head.

"Just think of it like you're paying me in sleep," she said. "That's worth more than a paycheck."

"Okay, Anna. You win," he said, smiling thinly, worried for her health. "Just keep both feet on the ground."

Anna went to the maintenance closet, hanging spray bottles and rags over the rim of the wheeled trash can, tucking a dozen trash bags into the handle. Then, beginning on the second floor, she worked her way to the basement, pushing the trash can alongside. Emptying bins, wiping shelves, scratching glitter and glue from nursery tables with her fingernail, dipping scrub brushes to scour urine stains from toilet rims. Bending close to dry them with a towel hanging from her waist, thinking: no messenger is greater than the one who sent him, no servant is greater than her master.

SIMEON KNEW ALL OF THE FAMILIAR FACES in the congregation: mothers with children, fathers who hung back, teens bunched together with their hands in their pockets, young men and women in jeans and flip flops. So right away he noticed the new face, the boy at the back. Seventeen or eighteen, with a wide nose and the lobe of one ear split and scabbed beneath a Band-Aid. Simeon had watched him throughout the service, rising a half-beat behind the others, groping for a hymnal. When the congregation lined up at the communion table, he came too; waited his turn, then stepped forward with his hand outstretched, palm down. Simeon raised a paper-thin wafer toward him, but the boy shook his head.

"What's the matter, Mister Reverend?" he said aloud. "Don't you want to shake my hand?"

Simeon took the hand and felt a folded piece of paper pushed into his palm.

"I believe in fair play," the boy said. "That makes me the better man."

Simeon watched him sidestep the table and go out the back door, wanting to rush after him, catch him by the shoulder and ask what he meant, but row after row of people were coming forward. Only much later, after the sanctuary had cleared, did he unfold the note again.

Between twelve and two tonight, the note said in pencil, *be ready.*

Simeon creased the piece of paper across the middle, a new crease, as if he were folding and weakening the paper to tear it.

At eleven thirty, Simeon closed his book and pushed it under the bed, out of sight behind the hanging sheets. After six months, his apartment held little more than a few changes of clothes and books scattered everywhere – under the bed, on a shelf at the small window, on the toilet tank. He lay for a moment on the crinkling mattress, dangling one foot off the edge, then went up the unlit stairwell into the church. In a kitchen behind the library was an automatic coffee machine; it chugged, filling a disposable plastic cup so hot that the plastic shaped to his fingers.

Outside it was dark weather, hovering between rain and snow; the air was blued against the buildings and the low, pregnant clouds. Wind whipped the boulevards, a chill that Simeon saw before he felt it, tumbling up the street, kicking leaves and bits of plastic. He turned sideways to the cold air so it would hit as little of him as possible, sidestepping alongside the buildings and pulling the collar of his sweater high, his stocking hat down, so only a thin bit of his skin was visible.

Simeon loved to walk the frost-slick streets at night,

despite warnings from Braxton that the neighborhood wasn't safe. The world unrolled like a grid in front of him, straight stretches of road, at every intersection a simple choice of left or right. He could veer and redirect, walking through the dead silence of downtown to explore rocks along the river or dark parking lots sunk beside the road, stand in trickles of heat coming through cracks around the shuttered doors of street-level offices, seek out the smells of cooking that seeped from apartment windows two floors above.

As he walked, he passed buildings with names chiseled into the cornerstones: entrepreneurs and philanthropists and politicians. He thought of his own name in block letters and shuddered; Simeon liked the idea of being a nobody, of invisibility – the second superpower of every child's dreams, after flying. He had left seminary for the Army, becoming not quite a private, not quite a chaplain, something in between. Then left the Army for the pulpit, a place that most people ignore. And for those few who did listen, he was duty-bound to point away from himself, past himself, to a God so big he couldn't be seen.

A car passed, its breeze quivering the air around him. The driver's window was open an inch, the tip of a cigarette poking through, and Simeon wished for a moment that he was a smoker, too. There is something about a cigarette burning in your palm, he always heard, that brings the world to you; you walk down the block and someone stops you for a light, or to bum one that will ease their quitting cravings. When a car passes in the cold with the driver's window cracked, you know the feeling; you have done the same thing a thousand times, and you can lift your hand to wave.

He doubled back up Main Street. The bank square, the

stores and businesses around were all dark and shuttered, except for the bright incandescent windows of the grocery next door to the church. Must be up late doing inventory, Simeon thought. As he crossed the church's lawn, the light from the grocery dimmed into a line of yellow, then disappeared.

He walked up the steps onto the church's front porch and took a deep breath, then pulled the brass handle as quietly as he could. Anna was there, at the piano, her back to him, her hair swinging side to side, marking time. He sat for a full minute, watching her and trying to block the wind coming through the doorway, afraid that closing it would make too much noise. But she turned and saw him anyway.

"Anna," he called, "I didn't know you play."

"I'm just messing around."

Her fingers floated above the keyboard without pressing down. The sanctuary filled with heavy sweet smells of day-old flowers and citrus cleaner as he came up the aisle toward her.

"You should lock the door if you're here late. It's not safe."

"I never do, and I'm here every night."

"The nights you can't sleep."

She laughed a sound like a cough, like dry leaves. "I never sleep, Simeon. I clean, then wait at the grocery store until you lock up then come back. Except for the nights you sleep in the pews."

He wondered if she had stood over him, looking down at him as he was stretched out in the sleeping bag, his mouth gaping, snoring.

"I heard Braxton mention a doctor," he said, changing the subject. "Maybe you should go."

"I went, there's nothing wrong." She brushed hair from her face with agile fingers.

153

"Sorry," he said. "You'd be surprised what people come to talk to me about. Often as not, they just need a vitamin and a nap."

She frowned and tapped her forehead. "Or maybe you meant a different kind of doctor."

"No, no. I didn't mean that."

"I went once. The whole time, I couldn't stop feeling bad for him," she said. "All those people lined up in the lobby, waiting to be fixed. But I blame him. A doctor should heal people, not just make them feel better. Even the word sounds like a lie, psy-chi-a-trist, all those consonants pretending to be soft, sheltering sounds."

Simeon pictured her on a leather couch, glowering.

"And anyhow, I could never make him understand what I was feeling. Most of the time I can't understand it myself."

"Feelings are funny like that."

"I don't think feelings are the problem," she said. "I think we don't know how to tell them, can't find the right words. Though words must come easily for you, being a priest."

"I'm not a priest, Anna. A priest is a holy man, someone set apart. I'm just a man, a pastor."

"Priest, pastor," she said. Then she hesitated, staring at the piano keys. "Can I ask a question, Simeon? One I've wanted to ask for a few weeks."

"Anything," he said, thinking – anything. He came around the piano, leaning on the enameled wood with his elbows. She touched the keyboard without a sound.

"Why don't we have a better word for God? It's such a funny word, small as a sneeze, too manageable."

"What would you call him?"

"I don't know. Once upon a time, his people were afraid to say his name at all."

"Maybe they were more scared of themselves, than of him. That they would say it wrong."

"I don't think so. I've never loved anything without being afraid of it, too."

Simeon thought: so do I, so am I.

"And I am afraid of him. Afraid even to talk to him, that he'll hear me and take notice. I'd rather fly under the radar with the secret joys and shit that keep me awake at nights, thinking: glory, hallelujah there must be a God. And then praying that if there is, he can't see what I think, what I want," she said. "Every morning when I wake up, I curl under the sheets just to feel them tented over every inch of me, like a second skin covering me. And I wait, and wait. I don't even know what for."

"Sometimes we find God in small places, Anna."

"I'm not scared that he might meet me in the corners,

Simeon. It's his bigness that scares me. That he only fits into wide open spaces, that he himself is a wide open space, like floating, like falling."

She stood up from the piano and Simeon picked up her coat, holding it so she could slip her arms in.

"Waiting is always lonely, Anna. But often, when you open your eyes, you find you aren't alone."

"You sound like a priest to me."

She half-smiled at him. The irises of her eyes, close, were brown overlaid with a faint sunburst of yellow, pollen spreading on quiet water. As they walked up the aisle of the sanctuary together, he found himself wishing with each step that she would stumble, that the carpet would reach out and grab her foot so he could catch her. When they reached the front door, she rested her hand on the handle and turned toward him.

"I want to whisper his name, Simeon. But I can't. Will you pray for me?"

But Simeon was watching her lips. So round in thought, lightning lips, illuminating the night in their thundering glory.

"It's dark outside, Anna," he said, enunciating carefully, wanting the words to be perfect. "I could walk you home."

"You know the streets are lit," she said but Simeon, bending at the knees and angling into her, found her mouth with his. His mind raced with doing it right, thinking hard, trying to be strong and soft at the same time. She leaned away, pushing back against his chest.

"You shouldn't," she said.

The door closed between them and Simeon's forehead dropped against the window set into the wood, its fragile cold within the circle of his cupped hands, his breath fogging everything. He wiped it clear to watch her walk past the dark storefronts, her chin lifted, her mouth moving. Then she tripped, sprawling to the pavement.

Simeon was halfway across the lawn when he saw Braxton hurrying out of a darkened doorway across the street. By the the time they reached her, Anna had pushed herself up to sitting. Braxton crouched behind her, supporting her head with both hands.

"What have you done?" he said, his breath short. "It's a good thing I was watching."

"Please, Braxton, just help me get her up."

"Stop it, I'm fine," Anna said.

The lights of the grocery lit the scene, the OPEN sign bright in the window.

"We can take her there. Get under her arm."

But Braxton would not reach under Anna's arm to support her, and slapped Simeon's hand away every time he tried to wrap it around her middle. He groaned, bending his hips and body away from her as he struggled to help Simeon lift her, at arm's length. Once she was on her feet, they walked together to the door and knocked until the grocer came around the counter and unlocked it.

Inside, Anna dropped into a chair with her elbows on her knees. The front of her coat was caked with mud and slush; her hands balled deep in her pockets, the knuckles jutting four pointed mounds through the fabric.

"Stop staring," said Braxton, wiping his face with his sleeve. "Anna, are you all right? When did you last eat?"

She shook her head, and the grocer reached into his glass case, passing a hard boiled egg and a glass of water to her. She drank the water. Drops of sweat beaded the egg like a jewel.

"Bless you for that," Simeon said to the grocer.

"Hmph," the grocer replied. Simeon knew the man. He had come to Sunday services for a few weeks, stopping at the front door each week to complain about the building. Swearing that when Mrs. Moffatt died, he had been in negotiations with her, to buy the lot to expand his store. Once, Simeon heard him talking, loud and angry, in the foyer about the lawn service, loud enough for others around to hear. The week that the final doorknob was fitted and the final hymnal slotted into a pew, he told Simeon that he would never come back, making a gesture of washing his hands. Simeon bought groceries at the man's store once a week, to support his business, but always wondered if they spat on his cold cuts when he wasn't looking.

"Anna, are you all right?" Simeon asked.

"Don't touch me."

"I didn't, I won't," he said, thinking – never again.

Her head jerked toward him, the colors in her eyes swirling, yellow and brown now a supercell over dry and cracked landscapes.

"You don't understand, Simeon. I'm saying that you shouldn't. I'm a stain spreading from person to person, dumbly fouling everything."

"No. I am," Simeon said, his voice so low that Braxton bent between them to hear it. "I thought you wanted me to, Anna. Or wouldn't mind, or I don't know. All that talk about not being alone."

"I was talking about God, Simeon. We were supposed to be talking about God."

"I was. But I was talking about me, too."

She cracked the hardboiled egg against the edge of the chair and rested her arms on her thighs, peeling the egg and dropping strips of shell clicking onto the floor. She broke it and ate half, listening to the sounds of them watching her, desperate to ignore them.

"I'm sorry, Simeon. You're not enough for me. There's no room under my sheets."

"Now hold on just a minute," Braxton said, shouldering forward so his body blocked Simeon from seeing her. "We can't have any of that."

Simeon elbowed him aside. "She doesn't mean it like it sounds."

"But what if I do?" Anna whispered, stronger than shouting, her voice filling the store. "Did you think of that? If I pulled you into my bed, would it make it any better?"

"That's not what I wanted," Simeon said, recoiling like a gun butt was held in close against his shoulder, the muscle absorbing the kick, bruising deep.

Anna thought of the nights that she would creep upstairs from scrubbing, to sit on the floor and watch Simeon snore on the pew in his sleeping bag. Her back against the pulpit, she would arrange and rearrange the puzzle of the day, sorting through moments one by one against the background of his breathing. His snoring was mumbled, gruff and yipping, but its angular edges were smoothed and softened in the towering space of the sanctuary so when it reached her it was dry and soft, with hidden melodies, almost a womanly sound. She would close her eyes into its ebb and flow, sounding out the space it shaped in the air so she could slip inside. When they passed each other in the hallways there was always a choreography in the way he spoke to her that made her want to move toward him, to let him take her in the crook of his arm, let him tuck in behind her, safe as a brother.

"I only wanted to be with you, close to you," he said. "I didn't want to hurt you."

"You didn't hurt me, Simeon. You made all of my suffering disappear."

"That's a good thing," Braxton said, edging in. "So this is over."

"Of course it's not good," she said. "Now I'm not angry, I'm not even scared, I'm not anything." Glancing down she noticed that she was still holding half of the egg. "God, I hate tripping," she said. "It's humiliating, it hurts."

"Nobody likes tripping," Braxton said, nodding sagely.

"But maybe I should. Isn't that what saints do? Live a life of hurt and humiliation, then wait for God to save them."

"God doesn't want you to suffer," said Braxton.

"Lovers never do."

"It's not like that, Anna. He's not like that."

"How are you so sure, Braxton? I want to be as sure as you. I can't think of a single thing that you say God wants, that's supposed to make me happy, that does. Why can't your songs and prayers make me happy? Your beautiful building? Why can't I say, maybe this is what love looks like?"

"I've watched you singing in the service," Braxton told her. "You look so joyful."

"That's not joy," she said. "How can you talk about joy, in a world so bent on beating people down? You talk about joy, but I say that if your God is worth believing at all, it's because he came into a beat-down world to be beat down with us, for us."

"Anna, you can't say such things," said Braxton.

"Why not? Does it scare him?"

Simeon stepped in front of her, pushing Braxton out of the way and kneeling in front of her chair.

"Anna, what can I do?"

"Don't do that. Get up," she said loudly, closing the other half of the egg in her grip, the white and yolk crumbling together in her fist. "When a man kneels in front of a woman it's to own her, or taste her, or worship her. Don't you dare, Simeon. A priest should never kneel at a woman."

Simeon was suddenly aware of the others — Braxton, the grocer, a boy behind the counter, staring at the two of them in a tableau, a mockery of a tableau, a cartoon of desire. He glanced around at them, muttering, "I'm not a priest, you know. She shouldn't call me that."

She suddenly shouted at him, "I'm not going to call you anything, Simeon, not anymore. Why can't you get that?"

"You tell him, sister," called the grocer from behind the counter.

"Anna, I don't know what to say."

"Good," she said, and reaching with the crumbled egg in her hand pressed it hard against Simeon's face, smearing it across his cheek, over his mouth and chin, down the front of his sweater. A slow, bright path of color across him. She sat looking for a moment, then left. As the door closed behind her, a woman caught it and came into the grocery, purse in hand.

"Are you open?" she asked.

"Oh what the hell," said the grocer. "What can I get you?"

Simeon and Braxton watched through the door as Anna retraced her steps up the front porch and into the church. Behind the counter, the boy switched on a whirling meat slicer, letting it spin to high speed with one hand on the tray. Simeon noticed, for the first time, a Band-Aid covering the split lobe of his ear.

"Hey son," the grocer called loudly from the register. "What do you tell a preacher with two black eyes?"

"I don't know, Dad. What?"

"Nothing. You already told him twice."

The son didn't laugh. Looking backward over his shoulder at Simeon, he heaved a ham onto the tray and pushed it toward the spinning blade.

THE WINE FILLED SIMEON'S MOUTH. He and Braxton sat in the back pew, passing an open bottle between them. From time to time, pale headlights swept the walls like shooting stars. At ten dollars a bottle, Simeon thought, there must be a dollar fifty left in this one.

"You stink like a fart," Braxton said. "Go wash that egg off."

Simeon shrugged and tipped the bottle again, pouring as much into his mouth as his throat would take in each swallow. Anna was at the piano in the front of the sanctuary, her hands folded in her lap.

"Girl like that, I can't blame you for trying," said Braxton. "But your mistake wasn't kissing her. It was not following through." He mimed a golf swing. "Finish it, man. Put a ring on her, put her in the backseat of a car and have a baby. If I were younger, I'd do it myself."

Simeon held up the bottle like an obscene finger.

"Or don't, I don't care. Give me that note again."

Braxton unfolded the note on the pew beside him, smoothing it, his eyes roving the paper.

"You know why this is happening, Simeon? God is in the neighborhood now, and people are angry about it. Look around you," he said, running his hands through his hair so it scattered like thoughts around his head. "We built big and we built beautiful, a place they can't disregard. Everywhere I look, I see that Anna was right – this is what love looks like." He tapped the taser, a small, square shadow in his lap. "God will bless it. He wants us to protect it."

"Don't say that out loud," Simeon said.

"You going to stop me, Army boy? You can't stop me, you can't stop God. Today's judgment day."

"But what if you're wrong?" Simeon asked, wanting to believe it. "What if something good is coming?"

"You pray your way, Simeon. I'll pray mine."

From her seat at the piano, Anna heard the word and thought – I can't pray, I've lost the thread. She stared at the mute keys, the tiny hammers poised to strike strings stretched to breaking, thinking about the unending rush of feeling in the world and how most of it never sounds. How most of it withers without ever growing to full fruit, without ever being tasted.

Unlit, the room seemed enormous around her. The exposed beams of the ceiling were reversed out like gashes in the sheetrock. The only real light in the room came from two electric candles set on each side of the pulpit – tall, thin, twin plastic tapers topped with flame-shaped bulbs enclosing an orange filament that danced up and down, faking fire. The candles embarrassed Anna; she thought them kitsch. She had once hidden them in the back of a maintenance closet, but Simeon found them and set them out again. He told her that they had been given to the church by a woman from Brazil, whose husband had made his name in Osasco as an amateur boxer. At thirty-five, he needed better medicine for his seizures, so they came northward to America. She gave the candles to the congregation on the first anniversary of their arrival in Chattanooga, telling of unwrapping them from a stained towel nightly in shadowy bus stations, to have enough light to wash her children in a water fountain. Pretending to blow them out and light them again with her finger, to giggle them to sleep. Then, licking her finger by their light, to carefully examine the forged passports for hints of dust and scuffs. The one thing, mile after mile, that they knew was coming was the ritual search for the wall outlet, the unsteady light on the walls as they drifted to sleep. The rest was pure hope.

As Anna sat at the piano, the candles suddenly struck

her as beautiful. Their light dripped orange onto the simple tablecloth and silver cup. Onto Simeon, flickering. The longer she sat, staring, the more their loveliness swelled and tangled in her. She thought of people lined up at the table, week after week, jostling as they shuffled forward together, toward bread that is bread but also flesh, wine that is not tears, but blood. In the empty dark of the room, the orange light hovered over the table like a breath, and she whispered, "Oh, my God."

Simeon heard her and called out, "What's that? What did you say?" but his voice was so jumbled in his mouth that he could hardly understand himself. Braxton grabbed his arm and pulled him back to sitting.

"Easy, tiger," Braxton said.

Simeon worked his mouth, but it only opened and closed. He thought: She might have been asking me again, and I could have told her different. I could have told her that if God can see through a bedsheet then we never have to be afraid, that if God can know everything then we never have to be alone, that if he can do anything but does good things instead, then maybe I can, too.

"Ask me again," he called to her, but it was nothing but a slurring groan.

"Don't fall asleep," Braxton said. "We have to stay ready."

But, I am awake, Simeon thought.

SIMEON'S FEET KICKED out in front of him in a spasm. He wiped his chin and looked around the room. His head felt like it was full of wet wool. Anna wasn't at the piano. His watch said one o'clock.

From behind him the noise came again: the front door scraping the tile of the foyer. Two shapes came into the sanctuary, wearing dark clothes and pulling ski masks down over their faces, carrying backpacks and metal canisters in their hands.

Simeon slid down to lie flat on the floor. Braxton was stretched out beside him, asleep; Simeon took the taser from the pastor's lap, hiding it under the pew, then shook him faintly. Braxton woke immediately, silent and aware. From beneath the pew Simeon could see that Anna was hiding underneath the piano. He slid toward her, under the next pew, as two pairs of heavy shoes passed and stopped at the communion table.

The cup and plate clinked loudly as they dropped into the backpack, followed by the microphone.

"We'll give them to Uncle," one of them said, not whispering. "Think of it as back pay."

The other picked up one of the plastic candles, looked at it closely, then tossed it onto the floor, its electric wick sputtering against the carpet. They pulled back the table's white cloth and pulled out the case of wine. Corks popped.

One wandered out into the hallway, calling back for the other to come see, and Simeon began dragging himself toward Anna, pulling forward one pew at a time. He scuttled across the open carpet and under the piano with her as the back door kicked open and the two men came back into the sanctuary, grunting under the weight of a television. They sat it on one end of the table, picked up the metal canisters and started shaking fast, metal rattling metal. Then a thin hiss, as they spraypainted the front of the pulpit, back and forth.

"Write your name," one said. "Or better, write Uncle's. Then he'll send his green jumpsuit crew in to wash it clean."

"They can't do this," Anna breathed into Simeon's ear. "Don't they know God sees them?"

She was inches from him. He put his hand on her face, near her mouth, but he was watching the two figures. Flecked with overspatter, one was swinging on a curtain and trying to tear it to the ground; the other walked, unhurried, back and forth along the wall, spraying enormous letters.

And in the wild quiet, Simeon was thinking that, even now, if they showed up on a Sunday morning, he would welcome them. He stood out from under the piano, his fingers trailing tenderly from Anna's face. One of them saw him, without surprise, and reaching, pulled the ski cap from his head. It was the boy.

The grocer was looping curses onto the back wall. Not seeing that Simeon and his son were standing face to face, he called out:

"Hey son, what's the difference between a son of a bitch and a man of the cloth?"

"I don't know," the son replied.

"When a son of a bitch knocks you down he says, This is good for me. When a man of the cloth does it he says, This is good for you."

The boy and Simeon watched at each other, the air around them fat with wine and the sterile, synthetic mist of spraypaint. Simeon reached to rest his hand on the boy's shoulder.

"I try to be a good person," the boy said, his lip trembling. "I try so hard."

"So do I," Simeon said. "I know exactly what you mean."

They heard a tiny chink of glass from the front of the sanctuary and turned to see Braxton step into the aisle, holding one of the electric candles. The bulb cracked, its filament flashing in the open air. He raised a can of spraypaint from the floor and, holding it at arm's length, aimed for the stuttering spark. The aerosol erupted, a flame three feet long stretching from the candle. He came toward the boy, who stood frozen to the carpet, but Simeon stepped between them.

"Get out of my way," Braxton said. Simeon didn't move, didn't speak. Braxton came closer, raising the flame between them, and Simeon came quick to meet him. The grocer and his son ran out of the foyer and were gone, leaving the television and backpacks behind.

Braxton watched them go, scanning the sanctuary's the torn curtains, the spilled wine, the spraypainted obscenities. Then he looked at Simeon, his face a knot of sadness, and turned to the curtains, fanning fire until it caught and spread quick up the walls.

Simeon sprinted through the back door of the sanctuary and down the hall, remembering a fire extinguisher outside of the offices. Tearing it from the wall, he ran back to the sanctuary but Braxton had locked the door. He ran at it with his shoulder, and again, then lifted the fire extinguisher over his head and brought it down on the knob, snapping it off. As he watched it roll on the floor, he remembered the master key in his pocket. He fumbled the knob back onto its stem, carefully inserting the key until it turned.

The door swung open onto pillars of fire twisting up every curtain. Braxton was standing at the communion table, his feet squared, flames pouring from each hand. The white cloth twisted in ashes.

"They're gone," Simeon yelled at Braxton, as loud as he could, batting him forcefully away and aiming the wide nozzle of the extinguisher at the table.

"I'm not finished," Braxton shouted with both hands over his head, flames rising in twin columns. The melting plastic of the candles trailed down his fists. Simeon lowered his shoulder and, wrapping both his arms around the pastor's waist, came up under him, already running. The spraypaint cans bounced away behind Simeon's long strides as the pastor's body bucked forward, kicking and slapping Simeon's back with open hands, pulling hair. Simeon struggled up the aisle and out through the front door, tumbling down the steps onto the lawn. The cold air hit them and the pastor was coughing, his face shining with sweat, the melted plastic cooling and setting around his fingers. Simeon, lying on the grass, thought — why am I not sweating, why is my shirt dry and rough against my skin? He tried to sit upright but felt his head swelling, already twice its size. He ran his hands over the parched skin of his face, peering between his fingers, half-expecting to see a medic appear, hovering camouflaged close by, and thread a needle into a wriggling vein.

He stood and stumbled up the steps back into the burning church. The tiles of the foyer were hot under his shoes, the flowers wispy stems in their vases. He made his way into the sanctuary, shielding his eyes against the smoke, and up the center aisle. He crawled underneath the piano with Anna just as the first piece of ceiling fell burning at the edges, trailing glowing strands of fiberglass after it. It spun down to the pews, where it burst in a cloud of dust.

Anna shook his arm; he didn't know how long he had been there.

"Simeon, you have to get up," she said, urging him onto his feet and to the back door. They pushed against it but the knob had fallen out and rolled away. She scrambled up to the pulpit, pulling him after her, backing against the wall, against the ladder that led upward to the roof.

"The roof is never locked," she shouted. She wrapped his hands onto the rungs and bumped the soles of his feet from beneath, hurrying him. He found himself at the top of the ladder, watching his hands fumble with the clasp, pushing it open, pulling himself out onto the bare roof, gripping the thin black tar of each shingle as he inched forward. His stomach clutched under his ribs. The sky was charcoal. A circling wind pushed him over onto his side. He could feel the heat from inside the sanctuary through the roof.

"Anna, where are you?" he called.

She put her hands on his neck. His pulse was shallow. "Simeon, what's wrong with you? Why are your lips blue?" She was streaked with wet and smoke as she crawled over him and set his arms over her own. He gripped her from behind.

"Hold onto me," she said. "Simeon, you have to keep me from slipping down the roof," she coaxed, but really she was leading him, straddling the ridgepole, crawling together toward the steeple. He leaned against her hands, his body mirroring hers, her legs leading his forward. When they reached the steeple she pivoted him off of her, flopping him onto his back on the shingles. She climbed onto the steeple's short platform, pulling him by the hand with her, pushing him back against the painted wood.

Smoke streamed around them from the windows below. A car slowed, stopped. Houses opened onto voices, they could hear running. Anna grasped the knob of the steeple's maintenance panel and, leaning wide, looked down. She was framed by the wide span of the hedge, thirty feet below.

"Simeon, can you hear me?"

Simeon pressed his back against the steeple, grasping blindly for her arm, squeezing it too hard. Neighbors specked the street below, sirens ringing from the fire hall down the street. Anna came around him, pivoting her arm to free it, but she couldn't break his grip.

"We can jump, Simeon. We can make it."

"Don't," he said. Then his thumb hurt and he looked up to see that she was biting it; he still clenched her wrists.

"Simeon, listen to me, I've done it before. Only I should have pushed off, aimed for the hedge."

Leaning against the paint, he couldn't move his legs. The road was filled now with cars doubling back, groups of people bunched on the lawn. Someone screamed, pointing at them. Simeon held on to her as hard he could.

"Anna, I'm saving you," he said.

She stopped twisting against him and, suddenly slow, pulled in close. She raised onto her toes, arching her face upward to him. "No, you aren't," she said and her lips touched his forehead, lightly; then she coiled her hands around his wrists and, putting one foot on each side of him, flat against the steeple, leaned backward. Simeon leaned forward to catch her, and she pulled him off the ledge.

Anna's hair ballooned around her. Simeon's hands shook loose, flapping featherless at the air. Shouts from below were cut off in a surge of wind. The hedge expanded beneath them, growing in detail until it opened, fringed in soft green, to take her. Then it took him, too, the needles cushioning before the branches underneath knocked the wind out of his chest.

ANNA WAS SURROUNDED BY HANDS reaching into the hedge. She watched them come at her, arms bundled against the cold, lifting and shifting her, threading her between the branches. Simeon was already on the lawn, underneath a hole cut into the side of the hedge. They set her beside him. She spat red, her tongue feeling the edge of a broken tooth. Sleepy flakes of ash dropped like warm snow in the cold, soundless and slight. People in winter coats and pajamas surrounded them, hurrying from all sides to bring blankets and bottled water. A graying couple from the neighborhood, whom Anna recognized from Sunday services but whose name she didn't know, crossed the road as fast as they could. The man reached Anna first, wrapping her in a tattered quilt.

"You okay, honey?" the man asked, helping Anna to her feet. His wife folded a corner of the quilt to wipe her face. Taking her hand, they led her past the edge of the crowd, stopping by reflex at the street's edge to look both ways.

An ambulance spun to a stop and Anna turned back to look for Simeon. As she watched, someone pushed a bottle of water into his limp hand. Others pulled off his sweater and unbuttoned his shirt, others tugged at his pants, the white briefs coming off with them. They folded the clothes and bunched them under his head. A man removed his coat to cover Simeon's nakedness as they knelt over him, pulling in close with hands full of dirty snow, cooling his forehead, his heaving chest. Behind them, the roof dripped flaming drops of tar that splashed onto the grass. A window cracked and the wall around it folded and dropped, the bricks buckling. But as Anna looked away, it seemed to her that the bricks stopped short before they hit the ground, shifting to form new configurations in the air.

SWIM

Our mother drowns in Alabama, off a white sand beach. Gabby and I are wading knee-deep, hunting shells with our toes. We compare them side-by-side on flat palms before Gabby shouts "Back you go" and throws them winking into the surf. I lower mine slowly, waiting for the current to twitch them alive in my fingers, to whip them away. It's a long time before we notice that Mom is gone.

The police station is a big room of hard concrete and beat-up metal teachers' desks. Everything is dusty and everybody is wearing dark blue uniforms. A man is talking to me, swallowing over and over, his Adam's apple thumping up and down, and Gabby won't stop crying, her eyes and nose and mouth spreading dark wet across a woman's shirt. Out the window I see piers and restaurants, and families playing on towels spread out like blankets on the sand, and hotels with stacked balconies. Yesterday Dad told me that the prices of the hotel room go up as the floors go up, because they're selling views of the waves. I haven't heard Dad say anything since this morning.

The airline upgrades our seats to first class for the flight home. At the check-in, white people stare and whisper at us, like Arabs and airplanes can't play nice. I want to pull the hijab closed around my face, to hide my dark skin and eyes so they can go back to forgetting about us. But then Dad buys three tiny bottles of whiskey from the duty free, and people decide we must be good Americans, and stop staring. Dad pours the whiskeys into a plant when nobody is looking.

In the first class seats, Dad is soon snoring beside me with Gabby tucked under his shoulder, in tight, like dads always do. Inside the airplane everything is cool and dry, closed in. It reminds me of hide and seek, of the air conditioning vent under my bed.

The stewardess comes by wearing a suit jacket that is buttoned all the way up to her smile.

"You want a Coke, honey?" she asks, bending very close so not to wake Dad and Gabby. "It's free. It comes with the ticket."

I know better than to wake Dad up and ask if it's okay. He would say, things that pollute in large amounts in small amounts are haram. He would also say, look at the miseries whiskey has brought mankind, the sin greater than the profit. So says the prophet. But look at him now, three bottles gripped in his knuckles. The appearance of evil.

Maybe in first class the rules change. I want them to, because I've heard that Coke has caffeine, and I don't want to sleep, to dream about waves whitecapped for miles, about Mom winking at me from the surf, her eyelids tumbled shells.

"Will caffeine impair my judgment?" I ask the stewardess. Her face is soft under her makeup.

"What a big girl question," she says, and I can feel her words on my cheek. "You are a big girl, a strong girl. You're going to be okay."

We come home in the early morning, before the sun is up. We drive Broad Street with its Bradford pears and parking meters glowing like summer Christmas lights, past the new, bright and shining theater where we've never been, and the marble white buildings with long flags sighing in the dark. As we turn onto Central Ave I see yellow backhoes with unAmerican-sounding names being unloaded from their trailers. Crews have been digging through the street while we were gone, and chunks of black tar and dirt are piled like dog poo on the sidewalk. Men in reflective vests and hard hats are shading their eyes against the bright work lights, peeking into the holes they've dug as machines work the dirt, tick tock, a few feet deeper. Soon, all the cars in the neighborhood will back out of driveways for school or work, the drivers' faces swinging past the

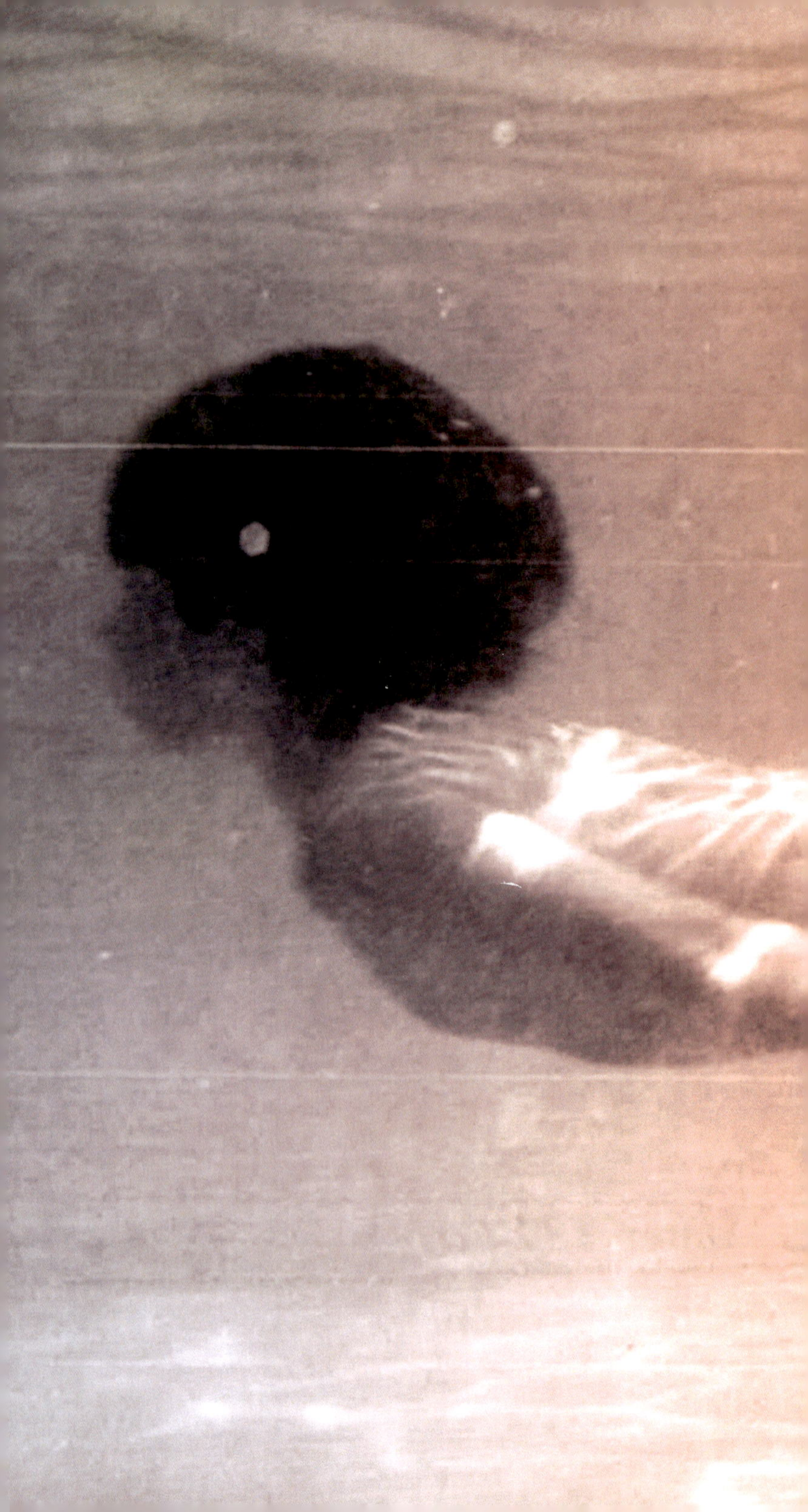

I don't want to sleep, to dream about waves whitecapped for miles

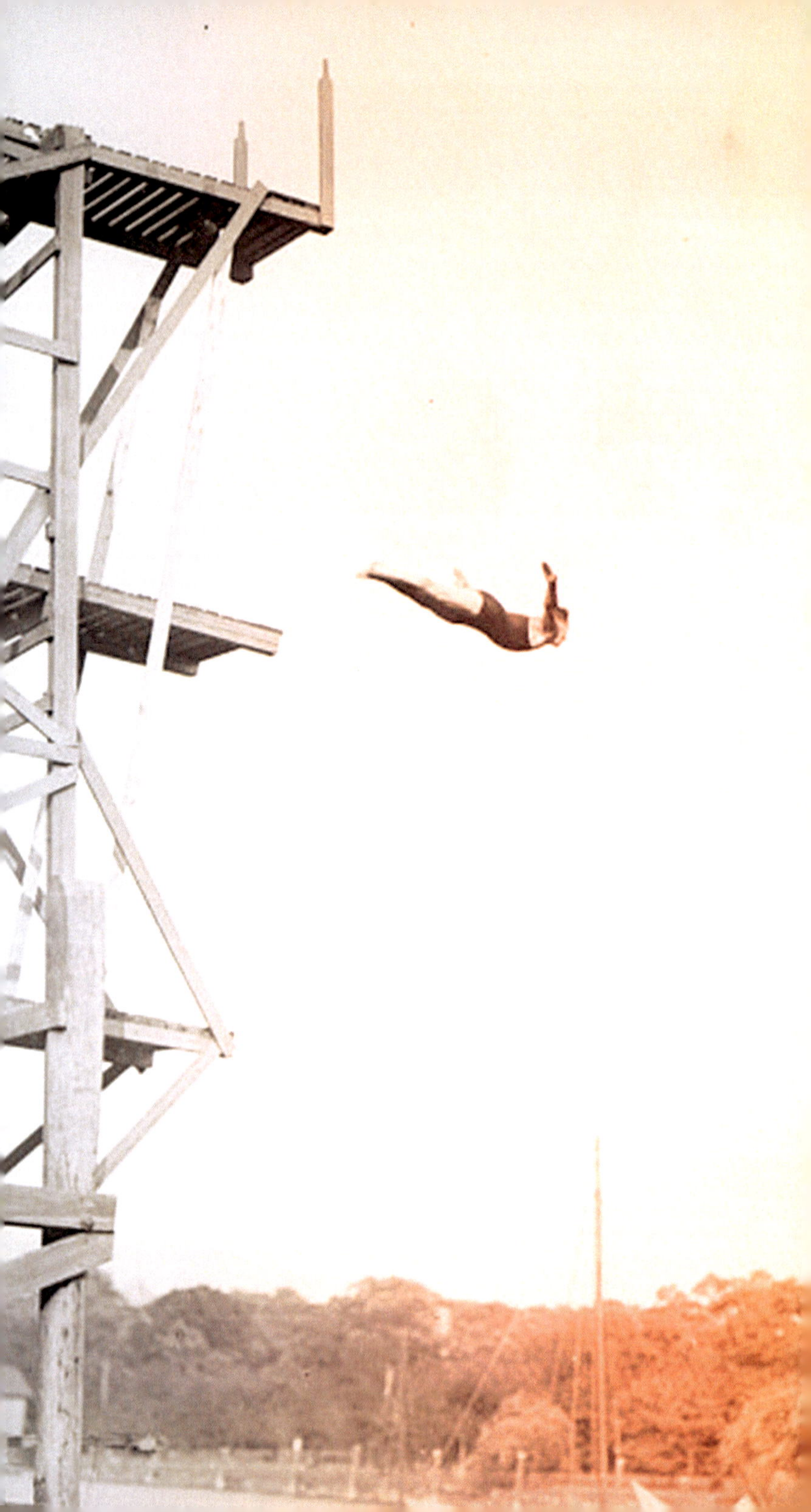

holes in the street, going slow, curious, stretching
their necks to see what is being buried or uncovered,
suspicious of everything.

In my room, I heave my suitcase onto my bed and fish
in my closet for my basketball. Out in my driveway,
the gravel grinds under my shoes. The cold light from the
work crews bends around houses, shining on the driveway
and the duct tape freethrow line, and the backboard
mounted high and rusting on the side of the shed.

Mom used to practice with me here. She was no good,
always out of breath and wanting a break, but she'd
reach around my hips, bump me, block my shots.

"You're not supposed to block your daughter."

"Says who?"

"But, you're the mom."

"Don't say, The Mom. How can I live up to that?"

I'd laugh and she would slap at the ball like she didn't
know how to steal it. I don't want to think about it, or
about men digging through the street, uncovering pipes.
About Mom coming apart slowly in the Gulf, bits of her
working their way upstream into Tennessee reservoirs,
to trickle under city streets. I want to imagine her
scattered in stars, reflected over the ocean. But I can't.

Dad appears in the kitchen doorway, rolling up his
sleeves.

"Sure you don't want to sleep a bit?" he asks me.

I bounce him the ball.

"Gabby won't either. And now your Teta is awake and cooking lentils, and saying we never should have moved to a city where we have no family to cook for us. The whole house stinks like onions."

I don't want to look at him, not now, unshowered and with his face unshaven, his glasses smeared, starting another day in the same clothes. He squeezes the basketball between his hands. I point at the rim.

"There are so many things for me to do," he said.

"Just ten minutes?"

We take turns shooting, the ball bright in the fake light from the street. My throws are all short but he rebounds for me, taking his big steps back to the taped line. At first he is clumsy, distracted, his feet blind on the gravel, but then the ball finds a rhythm with the sounds of morning – dogs barking, machines eating up the ground. I try hard to listen to his breathing between each bounce, the ball and breathing together in a way that seems to be saying something I can't hear over my own heartbeat. And then, as the driveway turns into day around us, he dribbles between his legs and steps back for a jumpshot. His feet lift off of the ground and the ball floats up his body, a still, spinless globe in his loose hands, up his palm, his fingers, the open sky.

It misses everything – rim, backboard, net – and bounces loud into a stack of garbage cans. He hops on one foot and says, "Fuck that," under his breath, "Fucking fuck." Then looks at me quickly, to see if I heard.

"What?" I lie.

"We better get inside. It's early, one of the neighbors will start shouting."

I scurry for the ball.

"You're pretty good," he calls after me and for a moment I think he might add, *for a girl*, but he doesn't.

"Thanks, Dad."

"I bet you make the team."

"I'm going into fourth grade. We don't have teams yet, not real ones."

"Oh, right. I mean, when you do."

We come into the kitchen. Gabby is seated at the counter. Teta's onions quiver the air over the stove as a vent fan tries to catch the smell and suck it out through the roof. It's morning, so Dad disappears down the hall, to kneel at the foot of his bed.

Yesterday morning, after breakfast, Mom had made us wait and wait before we could go down to the beach. Gabby and I whined and complained and squirmed until Dad said, "Doctors and their thirty minutes be danged," and Gabby ran across the room and out the screen door, with Dad chuckling behind her along the short boardwalk. I hung back with Mom, folding towels and hanging them over the backs of chairs.

"Remember these towels when you come in," she said. "It took hours for the rug to dry, last time."

Doctors and
their
...
...

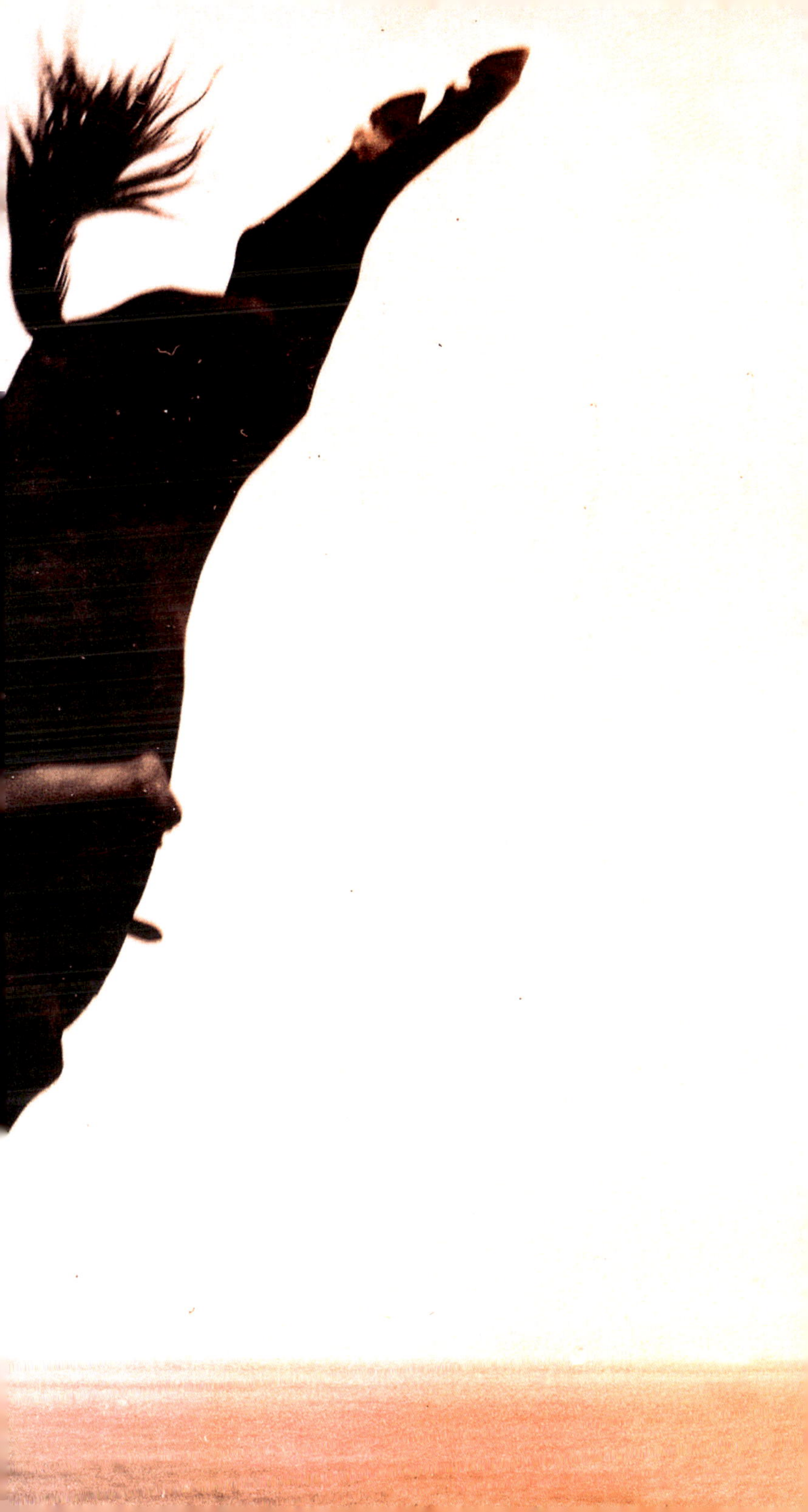

From where we sat, I could only see the top of Dad's head and the very tips of waves.

"Mom?" I said a couple of times. Finally she looked up. "Should we be swimming?"

She grinned and shook a towel at me. "You ask me now? After all that drama?"

"That's not what I mean."

All week long we had watched the TV set in the corner, its screen flashing pictures of oil on the water. Beaches spotted with globs like melted Hersey bars, miles of brightly colored floats trying to snake the waves clean while the rust-orange ribbons snuck swirling around them. Maps of the Gulf coast looked like Crayola nightmares, with bright and scary colors just off shore, coming closer.

"Oh baby," she said, her hands smoothing the towels. "The oil isn't to the coast yet, swim while you can."

"But," I started but she interrupted: "If I tell you not to worry, will you listen to me?"

"I can't help it."

Her hand stretched out, slow as time, to smooth the kinks in my hair. They bounced back under her fingers.

"I'll tell you what. I'll come down to the water in a little while, and I'll wade out past you, and spread out my arms to skim all of the oil back to sea."

"Okay, but if you do, the waves will just bring more," I said, laughing.

"Then I'll huff and I'll puff, and I'll blow it back like clouds," she said, blowing on my face. Her breath smelled clean, almost too clean, metallic and antiseptic from within the folds of her head covering. "I'll blow it to the north and south of you and Gabby and your Dad, so you can have a little more sun, a little more playtime."

I laughed again and crawled into her lap, just for a moment, before sprinting down to the surf.

Now, the next day, at the kitchen counter, Gabby's back is to me. Her hair brassy and brittle from the sun, still flecked with sand. I wonder why no one has tried to brush it out. Her chin is propped on the wooden counter, her arms hanging loose, her legs zig zags – as though someone set her down and, without arms to wrap her, she unraveled, waiting to be gathered together again.

Teta pinches saffron and salt through the air over the browning onions.

"We should do something fun today," she says, watching so the onions don't burn. "We can do whatever you want."

"What should we do?" Gabby asks.

"I think it would be a good idea if we went swimming. Would you like that?"

Gabby pushes at a knot in the counter that I never noticed before. She is going into first grade. She is so little.

"But Teta, didn't you hear?" she asks. "Our mother drowned at the beach."

"That's not the same thing," she said, her words sizzling the skillet. "She wasn't swimming."

I don't understand.

"She had no business going in the water, child, not at ten milligrams of Ativan a day. She could barely move her arms." Teta doesn't look at us, doesn't turn. Nothing moves on her but the hand that stirs the spoon.. "Good Lord, baby, your mother had a cancer. Didn't you know?"

I didn't.

"Fuck that," I say under my breath, so nobody can hear me but me. I put my arm around Gabby, my sweat cooling on my shoulders, mixing with the salt smell of the kitchen. I whisper in her ear, "Unfuck that."

Gabby looks at me with little big eyes, then hops down and runs up the hall. I follow after her to dig into my suitcase for a brush, then into her room to sit beside her on the bed. Then I help her on with her shoes. As she is struggling with the knot, the loop and roll around her thumb, I lean against her, silently measuring my arm against hers. Anyone can see that mine is much longer, maybe even long enough to spread out north and south, to make a space of sun for her to play, yesterday forgotten like clouds.

All the Way to
LAX

....

The reason that Johanna, at 23, was still a virgin was because of her grandmother. On Johanna's twelfth Christmas, the old lady had pulled her aside, brushing the hair back from her ear to whisper that the first time a woman takes off her clothes in front of a man, she always breaks wind. Loud and clear as a foghorn at dawn - the Big Bang, she called it. Of course, in her case it might not happen, her grandmother said as she disappeared into the crowded family room. But all through school and university, every time poor Johanna held a boy close in a dark corner, she clenched her backside tight.

On her wedding night she told Thomas, asked him. Said she'd spent her teenage years watching scenes of young love in movies, the television volume turned high as it would go, waiting for the telltale rumble. But she could never be sure. Was that noise a bedspring? A bass note in the sound track? Focused on the boy's face on screen, waiting for his nose to crinkle.

Thomas told her that he wouldn't care, that he didn't care. But she only wanted him to say it wouldn't happen.

"So let's find out," he said, laughing, already naked and fumbling at her clasps. Her face flushed upward from the neck and she pushed him sprawling out of the bed, backward onto the floor. She laughed, too, as if a string linked her laugh to his, pulling it out of her. But she also reached wildly and, finding the alarm clock, threw it at him. The plug jerked out of the outlet as it flew, its undulating cord trailing through the air toward him. He watched it come, still laughing, rolling out of the way as it smashed against the wall in a scatter of plastic and metal coils. That was one week ago, in a hotel room a block from the church, one hour after the cake and best wishes and rice floated in the air around them.

It is three o'clock in the morning and Thomas is standing at the open window of a Guangzhou hotel room in his underwear, watching through the trees of the garden for glimpses of crowds. Over the city's chatter of two-stroke motors and all-hours construction and the animal screeches of bus brakes, the chanting from the street rises and falls like a vinyl record spun fast, slow, fast against the needle. Johanna is on the bed, awake, wearing only Thomas' tee shirt. She keeps saying that the night could be more alive, faster, bolder, brighter if they were out in the streets too. The more people, the more possible; but here in the hotel room, there are only two of them.

Thomas' face grows hot despite the breeze coming off the high garden waterfall.

"Isn't that the point of a honeymoon?"

"It's one of them," she says. "But would it kill us to go out?"

"It might, Johanna. You heard what the concierge said. For God's sake, they put guards with guns at the door. They're trying to protect us."

"They just don't want the hotel's name in the papers," she says. "You can protect me. I could ride on your back."

"Like a mule."

"That's right. Like a big, handsome mule."

The air conditioning unit gasps, useless, from the window. Johanna sits up, her legs crossed off the bed like she is fishing in the carpet with her toes. She hardly looks up from her mobile phone, where her fingers sketch words and doodles on the flat illuminated screen. Her eyes follow the motion of her fingers rather than the effects they produce, and Thomas wonders if she is trying to lure him back into bed. But she is thinking about airline timetables and lost days.

"Our flight leaves tomorrow, eleven hours to Los Angeles," she says. "We could go to the Consulate, get them to help."

"Help with what? Sightseeing? And anyway, none of the taxis would take us."

"Why not? The news said only police cars and fire engines are being attacked."

"You don't know that's true."

"You don't know it's not."

She lies back on the bed, spread out like a treasure map. Her face is covered in tiny freckles, chocolate pinpricks on her skin like acne, or hives. Thomas loves to lie close to them, trying to decipher patterns and hidden meanings. She looks across the room at him.

"You got lucky," she says. "Stuck in a honeymoon suite while the world riots outside. Can't see the sights, can't go shopping. What to do? Okay, we did that. What next? We did that, too."

For a moment he thinks she is blushing, then he remembers the sunburn from every afternoon spent on the pool deck. Her shoulders going red, then tan, then red again. The night they arrived in China, the first attacks on the police took place a few blocks over from their hotel, and the doors had been locked since. Five days of the hotel's room service, of the pool. Wandering the gift shop, reception halls, dusty service corridors behind the kitchens where young men cut fish and vegetables for the buffet.

"But now you're stuck with a bored bride, and the room feels smaller than it did yesterday. It's egg frittata for breakfast again, and just because they call it a honeymoon, honey, doesn't mean it's always sweet."

She smiles at him, knowing that the ruddy tan looks good on her. Knowing that sweat and unwashed hair only highlight her lovely face, the power of the slow, focused tips of her fingers across the surface of his eyes.

"I'm ruining everything," she teases, tests. "We should just turn on the TV and become an old married couple, right now."

"It doesn't matter," Thomas says, thinking how when the Chinese say, It's nothing, it sounds like they mean it. All the stewardesses and salespeople and doormen chiming the words, dismissing gratitude. No need for thanks. It is my pleasure.

She stands and crosses to him, the cotton tee shirt draping and peaking on her. She presses against him, buries her face in his shoulder and bites, too hard, her teeth bunching his skin. Steps back to look where she bit, the wet hoop of teeth marks, and grins up at him. Then she suddenly looks out the window.

"What's that noise?" she says, as though until that moment she heard only her own voice talking. Through the window, from the trees and flowers and koi pond below, come little bursts like distant gunfire.

"It's tree frogs, remember?"

When the airport shuttle bus had pulled up to the hotel, the circle driveway was covered in the brown bouncing dots, their throaty rattling punctuated by the sound, every few seconds, of one of them popping under the tires. The doorman apologized in English, explaining that a long-time guest of the hotel had bought a dozen of the frogs in Hong Kong as a present for a local mistress; but she, saying that she wanted a child instead of childish gifts, had tossed them out the window. Within weeks, the frogs had filled the trees. The doorman said that every so often the hotel brings in chemical exterminators, but that the problem has become so bad that management fears they will have to close the hotel, to raze and rebuild the garden.

"It can't be frogs," Johanna says, listening to the harsh, reedy calls. "It doesn't sound like anything that's alive. It sounds like kids swordfighting with sticks, or a mob bashing police cars with rakes and brooms. Or guns out beyond the garden wall."

She peers through the open window, searching for a one-to-one ratio between what she believes and what she knows. The softness of the lamp hangs on her skin. The collar of Thomas' tee shirt is wide around her neck, the sweet sweep down to her shoulders, the collar bones pooling shadow. Summer tan in the night room, winter-white straplines peeking out. She sees him looking at her and pulls the curtain closed, stepping into him again. He puts his hands on either side of her face. She reaches upward to place her hands on top of his, guiding them up the sides of her face, over her ears to the top of her head. Resting his hands there, under her own, like a blessing, like an offering, like a claim.

He wears Johanna on his back, down the escalator and into the lobby. She is wearing sweatpants and a cardigan over the tee shirt. Her legs wrap him; every time she shifts against him she relaxes, trusting his grip, and Thomas thinks how she is smaller than she looks, easier to carry than he had imagined. He walks down the escalator, ignoring the black and yellow signs in Chinese and English that tell him to stand still and hold the handrail. They ride slowly into the bright lobby lights that come up fast to meet them, reflected from the polished floor and reception desk and the ten-foot sprays of plastic flowers. Hostesses smile in white collared shirts and black flats, the arches of their feet turning inward from standing all day under the gold leaf ceiling.

Even before the tea lounge slides into sight, Thomas can hear babies crying from the corner. A huddled group of parents, obviously American in their khaki shorts and print skirts, hold scrubbed and screaming Chinese toddlers perched on hips or bouncing on knees. When Thomas and Johanna checked in, they learned that the hotel offers special rates to Americans for a reason – hundreds pass through every year, staying at the hotel for a week while waiting to receive an immigration visa from the Consulate, for their newly adopted son or daughter. The front of the hotel is flanked with branches of US banks, shops selling disposable diapers and Cheerios; the staff specialize in Chinese lullabies and infant CPR.

Thomas treads across the gilt lobby with Johanna still on his back. The entrance doors are shuttered and hung with paper signs in English warning about the armed guards and 24 hour curfew. The American parents sit close to the doors, as if waiting for the Army to show up, while other hotel guests – in town from Frankfurt or Dubai or Chicago for trade fairs – spread throughout the tea lounge in champagne clusters of two and three, chatting up lobby prostitutes hoping for one more trick before daybreak. The Cantonese executives with them talk loudly, tonal and dogmatic even when discussing the weather, making the huddled Americans even more nervous.

Outside the night is warm, as it has been all week. There is music in the back garden, over the clacking of the frogs and the yellow tock of tennis balls from the lighted courts. Thomas sets Johanna down, her back to the buffet counter with its glistening croissants and frittatas, bright fruit and stacks of sweating bamboo dumpling steamers. On the wall behind the buffet is a fresco of simply stroked figures dancing in a row, women lifting their heels out of slippers, the black dashes of their eyes cut low, one hand stretched toward the next in line, never touching.

A bartender appears out of nowhere, hovering until they order drinks. Thomas runs his hand over the concrete tabletop. It is a dusty tint just missing white, smooth but indescribably dry, and he thinks that in spite of the artificial waterfall just outside the open French doors, and the thousand fountains in front of branded stores, and the wide proud Pearl River, the whole city feels dry. As if, as a service to tourists, giant unseen machines sucked it clear of all moisture. When the bartender brings the whisky soda, Thomas thinks that if he were to raise it over his head and smash it down on the tabletop, he could watch the concrete suck the liquid in - suck even the shards of glass like tiny pointed drops of water immediately away, leaving no stain.

Johanna elbows him softly, and points. In the corner, one of the couples is bent over a baby bundled to the eyes in a blanket. The woman cradles it, all of the color fading out of a crease in her forehead. The baby's face, what Thomas can see of it, is tightly wound, arched backward at the neck, stiff as stone. The father sits cross-legged on the floor in front of them, clapping his hands softly, trying to make the baby stop crying.

"You don't understand, Andy. How could you?" the wife says loudly.

As Andy takes the bundle from his wife, the blanket shifts and falls away from the child's face. A half-inch wide gap is missing out of its upper lip, with no gum behind. The flared red of the mouth folds neatly up into one nostril, and twisted teeth poke into sight on either side of the fluttering split, into the fluttering sound of its crying.

"That poor boy, his poor parents," Johanna whispers.

The wife is biting her lower lip; red skin dents white between white teeth.

"I wish I could explain it, Andy. It's like my own body is against me. You'd think after fifteen years, I'd be used to it."

"Maybe I could get you something."

"What would you get me? There's nothing for it."

"I don't know." The baby twists in his arms. "Maybe some Advil."

But she is beyond him, holding onto her wordless ache. She stands up and walks to the escalator.

"Wait, I'll come with you," Andy says, scrambling with the stroller and toys. The baby screams louder, its eyes and nose smearing across the cheeks and into the open mouth.

"No, you stay here."

Her hand is white around the handrail as she ascends backward, facing into the lobby. The escalator takes her past an open window and she waves her hand over the lobby. "And another thing, you're all full of shit," she shouts. "Don't tell me that isn't gunfire."

"They told us, it's frogs in the garden," Andy calls back, embarrassed.

"I don't buy it," she says. "Five days of riots, and now they've got machine guns."

"Not guns. Frogs," says a concierge from the desk, to everyone around. "A few years ago, they were very popular in Hong Kong, very exotic pets. If they bother you, shall I close the window?"

Thomas watches the woman disappear upward, but Johanna is looking at the baby's crying face. The father sees her watching and stiffens.

"Johanna, don't," Thomas whispers but she is already on her feet, walking toward the man. Thomas follows. Closer, Andy's face is as tired and blotched as the baby's.

"You two married?" Andy asks as they approach.

"For one week," Johanna answers.

"My wife and I have been for ten years. But I think it might be over." He sits down, the baby still crying loudly. He talks loudly in a lazy accent, as if he doesn't know how to talk quietly. "She wants a baby and can't have one. But she still gets cramps every month, so she thinks it's my fault. It isn't. I got tested." He points at the child. "So we did this, but I don't think she's happy with how it's turning out. My guess is she'll try with someone else."

Johanna smiles at him but he looks away from her, not wanting to receive it.

"You want to hear a joke?" he asks. "You know why we had to adopt a Chinese baby?"

"I'm sure I don't," Johanna says, playing along.

"Because two whites can't make a wong."

Johanna makes a face. "That's not funny."

"I know it's not," Andy says. The wailing is tremulous, twittering. "I thought of it last night, when he wouldn't stop crying, hour after hour, and I had to tell someone. I've always been like that, I can't sit on a joke, even a bad one at the wrong time." Thomas can tell that Johanna wants to wipe the baby's face, but she doesn't dare. "It's who I am. If people like me for me, great. If they don't, I'm sorry. I have good days, too."

"Where are you from?" Johanna asks.

"Why are you asking? You think I'm a racist. How could I be, with a Chinese baby?"

"No, really. I'm curious."

"Tennessee."

"Tell me about home," Johanna says, sitting into a chair beside him

The man tilts his head at her, not understanding. "What do you mean?"

"I don't know, I've never been to Tennessee. You tell me."

Thomas walks to the French doors, not wanting to look at this man, or his child with the too-wide spread of mouth.

"There's an island right in the middle of downtown," the man says. "Like it was dropped into the river, dead center between the north and south shores. It's really just a quiet outline of trees and muddy beaches, owned by a rich family until they gave it to the Mayor's office and he put their name on it, on the map.. As kids, we used to steal out there to throw rocks at tourist boats and skinny dip, out of sight."

"I bet loads of people saw you."

"Nah, nobody goes there but Scout troops and high school kids. We would hide the canoe into the droopy bushes at the waterline. My best friend had a telescope, and we'd watch life on both shores." He glances at the shining lobby clock. "It's nearly four in the afternoon there."

"Other side of the clock," Johanna says.

"Right now, men on restaurant verandas are dropping ice cubes into highballs. Mothers with strollers are crossing the walking bridge over the island. Wood knocks against wood as barges pass, farther out in the channel. On Saturdays at this time of year, fog rolls up the river and down from the mountains, my favorite weather. People sit in coffee shops, reading the Bible or Neil Gaiman. All the restaurants have empty tables. The air is wet and heavy. Raindrops. A bird."

"Your son will love it," Johanna says.

The man smiles back at her. "Before I was born, the foundries and railroads were booming. We had the dirtiest air in America, from all that coal and smelting. They say it never snowed, not even in the mountains. There was too much pollution, too much crap in the air for flakes to form."

"Maybe it's not the air that was full of crap."

He laughs broadly, patting the baby's back. "It snows now, don't worry. The foundries dried up and moved away, leaving downtown rusting and empty. But the air was cleaner. We could start building back better. Today, you can eat the snow."

Standing at the window, Thomas can barely hear them talking. As he watches through the glass, the water from the falls, fifty feet overhead, trails away and stops. The pond below drains in seconds, leaving orange and yellow koi flopping against the pond's plastic liner. A man in waders and a green hotel shirt, a long-handled net in his hand, appears and walks among the fish, scooping and flipping them into a wheeled tank. Another follows with a push broom, scrubbing away algae.

Thomas walks through the French doors, staring up at the empty waterfall, its artificial rocks and hidden pumps and gears. He steps into the dry pond, and the man with the fish net waves him back.

"No, no guests allowed," he says but Thomas replies, "It's okay, I'm okay." The man with the net shakes his head and returns to his business. Thomas crosses the pond bed and sees a path cut into the flowering bushes and sprawling ferns, leading down to the outer wall of the garden. An iron service gate is open to the street.

He turns and goes back inside, taking Johanna's hand and pulling her away from Andy, from the split and wailing mouth of the child, through the doors and outside.

....

On the path, the upturned leaves of plants are still misty from the falls. At first, the path looks empty except for bright and surprising shadows from the surrounding spotlights, but as they walk along it they see scattered broken pots and pieces of garden statuary, air-filled plastic bags of rotting fish, garden tools. Blue and white PVC pipes and hoses jut out of the ground. The flowering plants are taller than Thomas; they reach out to touch them as they walk. A lychee tree has dropped its fruit; it lies split and flattened on one side, the juice running, drying sticky.

They come through the iron gate and find themselves on a pedestrian overpass, over a six-lane highway. People are everywhere on the bridge and the road below, standing in the smudged windows of high rise apartments surrounding, twenty floors up. A few are lying down, wailing, for what Thomas doesn't know. A light post has been torn down, its wires splayed against the sidewalk, and groups of people shift in patches, flashlights bobbing in the dark ahead of them. Johanna holds tightly to Thomas' arm as they edge along the wall and climb onto stacked crates.

As their eyes adjust to the dark, they see a row of people standing on the concrete median, their arms folded. A hemp rope has been fastened to the railing and draped across the road. A dozen yards ahead, the crowd unzips around a man running with a rock in his hand, his arm cocked back. He lobs the rock out of sight over the crowd, then jumps onto a rusty scooter thumping alongside him and disappears. A wave of whistles and shouts goes up, with a scurry of clapping, then dies again into watching, waiting.

"Why are they so mad?"

"I heard that a policeman shoved a pregnant woman, during a crackdown on street vendors. She fell and is in the hospital."

"What happened?"

"Her husband fought back. They're migrant workers from another province. So are most of these people, come out to protest."

"I mean, what happened to her baby?"

"I don't know," Thomas said.

A man standing on the median holds up a penlight, a signal or symbol that Thomas doesn't know. Ahead, a semi trailer truck creeps forward, flashing its headlights. The crowd backs away in front of it, slows, and bunches upon itself. The truck rolls to a stop at the wall of bodies, idling, gunning its engines.

A man jumps onto its hood and smacks the windshield with an open hand. Another follows. The truck's horn blasts and the crowd folds around it like a closing fist, pushing against the cab, rocking it side to side, the headlights swaying, until its gears grind and it reverses slowly back to the far side of the bridge.

"Hell yeah," Thomas shouts, clapping along. "It didn't have a chance, not with so many of them. Have you ever seen anything like that?" A few of the people closest to him turn and nod, and he stamps the crate with his foot, rocking it, and shouts again. Johanna clings to his sleeve. The truck backs out of sight. The crowd lets it go, clapping and cheering. The air is thick with the sharp smells from the shops and alleys, with people breathing and yelling together, shouting things that he doesn't understand.

"I would have done the same thing," he shouts. "If someone pushed you down, with a baby inside you, I would strike back too. I would call everyone I know to come smack the hand that touched you."

"Thomas, please stop," Johanna says close into him. His head turns toward her and he sees her dim, faded face in the dark. "I want to go inside."

"But you were right, Johanna," he shouts back. "We'll be fine, we can slip into the crowd, be back inside in an hour. Nobody will know."

"You can't go without me, Thomas, and I won't go. What if I can't hold onto you?"

"You can. I can."

"But what if you can't?" She will not let go of the wall.

"Come on, Johanna. This is what you wanted."

"I don't want it anymore," she says. "I hate this and I'll hate you if you make me. I've got all my eggs in your basket, Thomas." She said it as if she didn't have a choice. "Please, just take me home."

She pulls him down off the crates and into the gate, closing it behind them. He lets her lead him up the path. Overhead, the waterfall comes back on, its first drops soaring through the air toward the shallow pond, so they have to hurry across before it fills. As they go, the hollow sound of the frogs springs up around them, and a web of reflected light from the water flickers across their faces.

....

Inside, the lobby is quiet. It is five o'clock in the morning and cleaning crews are mopping the floors with hand rags. The lights are dimmed. The American parents have gone upstairs to order room service for dinner, pizza or hamburgers, keeping their internal clocks set to U.S. time to avoid jet lag. With nobody to wake him, Andy is sleeping in the corner, tipped over on the couch. The child is crawling at his feet, trailing the blanket.

Johanna sits down and looks out the window, not talking. Thomas goes to the buffet and, with a paper napkin in his hand walks its length, opening warming plates to peek inside. He chooses a slice of frittata and goes back to sit beside Johanna. He cups the napkin under his chin, takes a bite and chews slowly, then another.

When he finishes, Thomas crosses to the buffet for another piece. As he sits back onto the couch, he sees the baby watching him. In a loose shirt and oversized drawstring pants, the child looks up from the floor, used to seeing the world from that angle, to playing with any shoelace that lays on the floor beside him. His face swivels, following Thomas' hand.

Thomas gets up. The child watches warily, out of the side of slitted eyes, without moving – as if he had learned to sit still to go unnoticed, or as if he were used to waiting until his own bubble of dark quiet. But as Thomas comes within arm's reach, he lifts his chin and opens his mouth, the lips spreading wider than any mouth should go.

Sitting onto the floor, Thomas pulls off a piece of the frittata with his fingers. The baby takes it in his hand and pushes it into his mouth, his whole hand following after it, trying to push the food back to the throat but missing. Thomas bends down, his head almost on the carpet, and sees the food drift upward, through the gaping palate, until the tongue works it out through the nostril.

Thomas lays one hand on the baby's head and wipes the egg away, flinging it across the burnished floor. He takes a bite of the frittata, chews it and spits it into his own hand, then, holding it tenderly between his fingers, pushes it into the child's mouth. The baby gnaws his fingertips and Thomas works by feel. His fingers slip up into the gap in the child's lip, the skin closing around it like a wound. The baby swallows and suckles at Thomas' finger, trying to draw milk from it.

"Hold on, fella. I'm not your mother," Thomas says and takes another bite, chews it. Andy stirs above him and sees Thomas crouching on the floor.

"What the hell?" he starts, angry, shrill. "What do you think you're doing?"

"Quiet," says a voice from behind them and Johanna is at Thomas' shoulder. He didn't know she was watching. "Don't say a word, Andy. Just watch."

Thomas pantomimes a bite, then chewing, then shows the small ball of mash in his palm. He reaches gently and sets it at the back of the child's teeth, then plugs the gap in the palate while he swallows.

"Like this," he says and hands the napkin to Andy, who comes to the floor beside him. Thomas and Johanna watch as Andy takes a bite and chews, stroking the boy's face before spitting the mash into his hand. He doesn't turn to thank them as they stand and walk away from him, breaking into a run halfway up the escalator. At the landing, they nearly collide with some men in suits, who step aside to avoid them. They come around the landing and onto the next escalator, now slowing, reaching for the other's hand as they run.

Martin Geyer stirs against the sheets. Through his narrowing eyes he seems to see sleep creep the room, swimming through the unmoving air to drop and smother the night away. He forces his eyes open, feeling that he's missed something.

"What did you say?" he says, reaching to touch his wife. After twenty-seven years of traveling to textile trade shows in Guangzhou, the first month of his retirement he has brought Beatrice to see the city he knows so well. He rests his palm against her thigh, the soft skin wrapped in a loose nightgown that warms quickly under his hand. "What was all that racket?"

Beatrice lays beside her husband, rearranging her body into a warm spot on the sheets.

"It was that young American couple. The ones who are always in the lobby in their pajamas."

"And I was hoping to sleep in late. Did they wake you, too?"

"Not really."

Martin shifts his leg so it touches her thigh. She moves her book to the night stand.

"The light on the landing is out," she says.

"We need to tell the staff. These escalators are dangerous enough as it is. Are they married? Is she his wife?"

"Who knows these days."

"But they're so young," he says.

"They wouldn't be the first."

She presses the soft underside of her foot against his ankle, and they both lay silent for a long time.

"But is everyone all right out there? I only heard a loud sound. Did somebody fall on the escalator?"

"No, nobody's hurt. Kind old man."

He moves toward sleep.

"I was up for a glass of water," Beatrice says, her voice slowed in tempo with his snoring. "I heard voices from the hallway and went to the peephole, because it's so early. I could see them standing in the dark. They were only a few feet away from me, breathing like they had been running, resting with one hand on the wall beside our door. I could see their shapes so clearly. He pushed against her, but not hard, like he was covering her, and she slipped her hand into his waistband. I looked away, afraid they might hear me, but after a minute I looked again. They hadn't moved. I couldn't make out their faces. Then suddenly, he bent and picked her up onto his back and began walking up the dark escalator, her legs swinging in the air as they went."

AUTHOR'S NOTE

On a project and a place

The First Time She Fell started a year ago, as an experiment. In my workdays, I collaborate with design agencies to articulate the voices of nonprofits, start-ups and corporations – bringing together verbal and visual meaning, in the hope of creating great brands. In mid-2010, I found myself wondering what could happen if we used the same tools to create fictional voices (that are true, but made up).

So I wrote eight short stories and set them in fringe neighborhoods on the edge of downtown, in my hometown of Chattanooga, Tennessee. Then I handed each one over to a different graphic designer, illustrator or industrial designer, giving them free rein to bring a layer of visual interaction and interpretation to the story.

All in the belief that creativity, though rooted in solo acts, grows with collaboration. That our ability to make something meaningful grows, rather than being stifled, when we create with people who inspire us.

When choosing collaborators, I looked for designers who have deep talent in their respective fields, who (like me) are under 40 years old, and who, early in their careers, spent time in Chattanooga. In recent years, six of the eight have moved on to Boston, Birmingham, Knoxville, Philadelphia and San Francisco. Another moved to London, then moved back. So as their designs came in, I wasn't surprised to see that many of them had shaped small moments, grounded in memories of life in our small city. What did surprise and delight me, however, is how much each story remains a love letter to place – sometimes sharp, but always tender.

So I trust that any reader lucky enough to know Chattanooga will recognize it, but also forgive my loose use of the map and tendency to invent locales. Similarly, while I know judges and ex-cons, pastors and prep cooks, daughters and fathers, the characters in this book, and the situations in which they find themselves, are all fictitious.

– cl, 2011

ACKNOWLEDGEMENTS

Where credit is due

To the incomparable Bessie Smith, for writing her 1928 masterstroke "Thinking Blues", which gave Bess every line of dialogue that she speaks in "Thin King Blues". "Cantata 82" is named for Bach's "Ich Habe Genug", BWV 82 in the Schmieder catalogue. To Rickey Lee Horne, for the childhood nickname Superchicken. To Lidewij Edelkoort for her thoughts on why we're hungry for comfort in the 21st century. In "East Coker", T.S. Eliot wrote the lines that shifted into "The Houses Under the Sea, the Dancers Under the Hill". The Georges Simenon books referenced are *Maigret*s; Neil Gaiman's is *American Gods*; the basketball scene in "Patete" samples James Baldwin's timeless description of Sonny on stage.

With thanks

First, to 8 remarkable designers – Michael Hendrix, Ben Horner, Mandy Lamb Meredith, Nick DuPey, Liz Tapp, Roby Isaac, Joseph Shipp and Beth Joseph – for my favorite collaboration ever (so far). To the super Paul Rustand for designing the cover and helping puzzle eight layouts into a book. Also to Dr. Mary McCampbell, Ali Burke, Lacie Stone, Robb Ludwick, Eliza Hill, Matt Greenwell and Phillip Johnston. To Tubatomic for helping implement 21st century word of mouth. Most of all, to Krista Gerow, Ada Matthews, Evelyn Jane and Mathilda Pinyi. And to the Lyndhurst Foundation, for a MakeWork grant that funded designer stipends and made this collaboration possible.